HONOR BRIGHT

HONOR BRIGHT

RANDALL BETH PLATT

DELACORTE
PRESS

Published by
Delacorte Press
Bantam Doubleday Dell Publishing Group, Inc.
1540 Broadway
New York, New York 10036

The trademark Delacorte Press® is registered in the U.S. Patent and
Trademark Office and in other countries.

Library of Congress Cataloging-in-Publication Data

Platt, Randall Beth.
    Honor bright / Randall B. Platt.
       p.   cm.
    Summary: While visiting her grandmother during the summer of
1944, a fourteen-year-old girl helps to heal the wounds that have
been inflicted upon three generations of women.
    ISBN 0-385-32216-X (alk. paper)
    [1. Forgiveness—Fiction.   2. Mothers and daughters—Fiction.
3. Grandmothers—Fiction.   4. Twins—Fiction.   5. Stepfathers—
Fiction.]   I. Title.
PZ7.P7129Ho   1997
[Fic]—dc20   96-21701   CIP   AC

The text of this book is set in 10.5-point New Aster.
Manufactured in the United States of America
April 1997
10 9 8 7 6 5 4 3 2 1
BVG

FOR MOM AND DAD PLATT

HONOR
BRIGHT

ONE

"Damn it, Theadora! Will you *stop* kicking the seat? I swear, you'll cause an accident!"

Theadora found her mother's face in the rearview mirror, then looked over to her brother riding next to her.

"How can my feet cause an accident when you're driving?" she asked.

"You know what a nervous driver I am! I jump a foot every time you shift your legs. Now, please!"

Theadora gave her brother an evil look, then purposely recrossed her legs, making sure to give the driver's seat just one more accidental thunk.

"Sorry," she said as she watched her mother jump, then stiffen.

"I mean it, young lady!"

"She did that on purpose, Mom," Howie, the brother, said righteously.

"I know she did. She just wants to do everything she can to make this trip miserable for all of us!"

"I do?"

"Yes, you do!"

"Oh," Theadora mumbled into her reflection in the window, "well, that explains everything."

Theadora Ann Ramsey was fourteen years old, cocky, angry and proud. She'd spent the majority of those fourteen years proving she could outrun, outsmart, outthrow, outdare, and far and away outdistance any boy . . . anywhere, any way, any day. She despised her mother, barely tolerated her brother and hadn't a true friend in the world. If it was Tuesday, she wished for last Sunday. If it was light, she longed for dark. If it was Oregon, she prayed for Siberia. If it was peace, she jockeyed for war.

To make matters worse, she was harnessed with bands on her buck teeth and was freckled mercilessly, and her head was topped with an unruly thatch of dark brown hair bobbed to the earlobes, then pageboyed. Added to all this awkward horror were two severely scarred, skin-grafted but perfectly functional hands. Ah, but there was nothing wrong with Theadora, preached her mother, that some serious time at the makeup bar in the corner drugstore couldn't amend. That, perhaps a decent haircut, eventually some red hair rinse and, oh, of course, gloves. No lady should ever be without gloves, Theadora especially.

Theadora, or Teddy as she preferred to be called, had been warned weekly by her brother that she'd require the unearthly talent of fifty fairy godmothers, working three shifts, just to elevate her to the status of ugly duckling. Not that Teddy cared. Gloves, henna rinse, makeup and fairy godmothers were for budding Cinderellas who required nothing more in life than monocled Prince Charmings to arrange things in their pampered, safe castle lives. She'd never bought the fairy tale, written, no doubt, by a man anyway. Jack the Giant Killer was more to her liking. She had dragons much larger to slay.

But her brother, Howard, had all the answers regarding his sister. Being six minutes older, he had the answers before the questions were even asked. Teddy was a drip, it was as simple as that. Not the carbon copy of their lovely, feminine, dainty mother that all daughters were supposed to aspire toward. A changeling, perhaps . . . yes, of course! Switched at birth! Either that or maybe Teddy was a little, well, mannish. What worried Howard about this theory was, if his twin had gotten a ration of his male hormones, then maybe he'd received some of her female hormones in the exchange. But chin hair was sprouting right on schedule, his voice was finally starting to drop an octave and very little could hold his attention more than a nearby set of fully developed breasts. Still, there had to be a reason Teddy was so strange. They couldn't possibly be related, except for the fact that Howard was a Y-chromosomed duplicate—identically tall, lanky, also harnessed with bands on his buck teeth, freckled mercilessly and similarly cursed with unruly dark brown hair, now butched all around for the summer.

Howard, therefore, had spent the majority of his fourteen years avoiding, ignoring and denying the existence of his twin sister. This arrangement suited Teddy just fine. She didn't have any more need for Howard than he had for her. That was the way it had always been . . . right up to their fifteenth summer.

———

Of all the places Teddy could have been that June of '44, the last place she would have chosen to be (including a foxhole in Normandy) was the backseat of a hot, smelly old Plymouth, limping down Oregon's Highway 30, battling car sickness, sparring with her brother, damning her mother. She took her gaze from the cow-dotted pasturelands and forced it on her mother's reflection in the rearview mirror. Always the vision of loveliness, her permed red hair frizzed out fetchingly from her hunter green scarf and waved playfully with the warm air sweeping through the windows. Her cheeks were flushed—or was it too much rouge? Each cheek was dotted with a perfect, deep dimple . . . each dimple was filled to overflowing with the secrets of countless flirtations. Oh, how men loved the dimples. Her face was dutifully dusted with powder, her large, blue eyes framed by bluish liner. Her mother's lips, no matter where she was, when or how she was, were always full and brightly painted.

Teddy watched her mother as she gripped the steering wheel with panicked determination, nose first, always alert to the potential vehicular devastation and accompanying front-page headline, "Mother–Daughter–Son Killed in Fiery Crash!" She smacked a wad of gum nervously, and she never once allowed her back to relax against the seat. It was a wonder the three-for-one obituary hadn't already been written.

Teddy returned to the journal on her lap and tried to concentrate on her last entry:

JE118—June 9—I hate this car! I hate the smell! What's worse? Cigarette smoke or Mom's cheap perfume? I hate this

whole damn thing! Why can't she just leave me out of this?
Holiday Beach. Where's that? What's wrong with Tacoma?
OK, plenty, but the whole crummy summer! Christ! Why
me? Just when things were starting to go right!

Her mother slammed on the brakes as she did each time
a curve, no matter how unthreatening, appeared in the
road ahead. Howard slid into his sister, and she shoved
him away to protect the privacy of her journal.

"Hey, take it easy!" he grumbled.

"*Now* what're you two fighting about, huh?" Dee Dee
Ramsey screeched from the driver's seat. "I swear to God,
you're both acting like babies and I can't stand it any
longer!"

Howard poked his sister and said, "Well, one of us *is* a
baby!"

Teddy seized his finger and gave it a wrenching twist. He
cried out in pain and retreated to his corner of the backseat.

"I mean it, you two! I'm going to get into a crash or a
nervous breakdown!" Mrs. Ramsey hollered, gripping the
wheel fiercely and not daring to look back at her children.

Teddy settled back to her journal writing but was soon
feeling backseat nausea rising inside her. She looked outside the window to take her mind off her mother's driving,
the agonizing curves, her brother's glaring, their impending
destination and the burger and fries playing rugby in her
stomach.

They were somewhere between Longview, Washington,
and Astoria, Oregon. All she knew for sure was the Colum-
bia River was on their right and the Pacific Ocean was

somewhere straight ahead. And beyond that, promised her mother, by sundown, Holiday Beach. Grandma Rose. Oh God.

She closed her eyes as the Plymouth negotiated a series of hairpin turns, each one able to roll a tighter curl than the last.

She felt her stomach tighten as they took another corner. *Don't brake,* she silently warned her mother. *Whoever gave you a license oughta be shot!* She furiously rolled down her window, leaned her head out and took a long, deep breath. She forced her eyelids to stay open against the wind until her eyes began to sting. . . . Tears rushed to soothe, but were quickly blinked away. She pulled her head back inside and warned, "Mom, I'm getting—"

"Light me a cig, will you, hon?" her mother asked, throwing a pack of Camels and a lighter back to Howard.

"No, he won't light you a cig!" Teddy retorted, seizing the Camels and shoving the cigarettes back. "Mom, we gotta stop. I'm gonna puke!"

" 'Gotta! Gonna! Puke!' Some talk!" her mother snapped.

"I mean it, Mom! Pull over!"

"Oh, all right. Hang on, I can't just stop here in the middle of traffic!"

Teddy looked behind them. Not a car was to be seen. "Hurry!"

"All right, Theadora. Deep breaths, damn it, deep breaths!"

"This wouldn't happen if you'd let me drive," Teddy snapped, in and out of deep gulps.

"Don't be silly. You're only fourteen. You can't drive," her mother shot back.

"You oughta check your odometer once in a while, Mom," Howie offered, giving his sister a threatening glance to spill more.

"Shut up!" Teddy offered right back. "I mean it, Mom. The least you can do is let me ride in the front seat!"

Her mother dared a quick glance at her daughter in the mirror and answered, "You know Perkie can't ride in the backseat!"

"Oh, great, Mom. It's okay if I get sick but oh no, not your precious little Jerkie! Mom, I'm warning you! My mouth's starting to water!" Teddy threatened, her hand on the door latch. As the car began to slow down, Teddy looked over the front seat at the Pekingese, perched arrogantly on a stack of fluffy pillows elevating it so it could see out the windows. The dog returned her look, growled up at her and followed it with a hairy-lipped "hih-hih-hih" pant that Teddy knew was Pekingese for "Go ahead and puke!"

"Better hurry up, Mom," Howie piped up. "If she pukes, I'll puke."

The car slowed to a cautious crawl, and after an obedient hand signal to absolutely no one, Dee Dee Ramsey pulled the car to a stop. Teddy was out and pacing, hands on hips, before the hand brake was set. She leaned over and emptied while her brother walked in the opposite direction, found a bush and peed.

Teddy was sitting on a large rock, taking deep, long breaths, when Howie approached her.

"I told you, if you'd stop eating, you'd stop puking," he said.

Teddy looked back at their mother, who was lighting a cigarette and walking Perkie.

"Look at her," Teddy said, watching their mother as she walked her dog. "Out here in the heat, middle of nowhere, dressed for an audition on Major Bowes!"

"You know why, don't you?" Howie asked, looking down the highway at an approaching truck.

"Because-you-never-know-when-Mr.-Right-will-come-along," Teddy replied, droning the words she'd so often heard from her mother.

The truck passed them, and the driver, upon seeing Mrs. Ramsey bending over to converse with Perkie, honked appreciatively. Howie watched the truck whoosh by, then said to his sister, "It's because she wants Grandma Rose to think she's doing all right for herself."

Teddy gave her brother a disgusted look. "You're so wrong you're pathetic! If that's what she wants Grandma Rose to think, then why the hell's Mom palming us off for the whole summer? She's probably going to hit the old lady up for a loan."

"She's too proud, Teddy. You're way off base!"

Teddy faced her brother and said solemnly, "Yeah? Well, I'll tell you something else, Howie-Cowie: She doesn't want us around Tacoma this summer because she's out to get a man and she doesn't want us to see how she does it."

Howie grabbed his sister's arm and said, "That's not fair, Teddy! Mom's doing the best she can with what . . ."

". . . with what she's got!" Teddy finished for him.

"Shut up before she hears you!" He looked back at his sister and added, "You're dead wrong about Mom. You always have been."

8

After the family was sufficiently aired, relieved and watered, they climbed back into the Plymouth, and returned to their separate corners. Mrs. Ramsey handed out lemon drops, added another layer of lipstick, signaled and pulled back out onto Highway 30. Once the lemon drop disappeared, Teddy surrendered to drowsiness. Before dropping off, she offered a brief prayer to St. Christopher, who she'd heard occasionally watched out for old Plymouths being propelled by wheel-gripping, overdressed drivers. Teddy waited for Howie to nod off to sleep before closing her eyes, her journal tucked safely under her.

TWO

Mercifully, Teddy didn't wake until the car came to a halt at a filling station in Astoria. Dee Dee turned around and woke Howie.

"We there yet?" Howie asked, still half asleep.

"Almost," Dee Dee answered. "We're in Astoria."

"Damn," Teddy muttered into her pillow.

"What was that?" Dee Dee demanded. "Now I told you, Theadora, you'll have to clean up your mouth around Grandma Rose."

"What the hell for?" Teddy retorted boldly.

Dee Dee grabbed her daughter's dungareed knee, pinched her glamorous nail into it and said sharply, "God damn it, I said watch your language, young lady!"

Teddy fixed her mother coldly with a stare and said, "Why should I? You swear like a sailor. Like mother, like daughter."

Dee Dee returned her daughter's piercing gaze. *"That'll be the day!"* She tightened her grip on Teddy's knee and added, "So watch it, huh?"

Her mother let out a dramatic sigh, took off her scarf and ran her long, pale fingers through her hair. "Look, I don't like this any better than you do, all right? You think I'm looking forward to this, you got another think coming."

"But, Mom, if it's because we need money, then why didn't you let me stay in Tacoma? I was all set to start work at the dairy and everything!" Teddy's eyes were starting to sting.

"No daughter of mine is going to work in some stinky, filthy cow barn! Now, it's final. The plans are all made. We're almost there," her mother added coldly. "Your grandmother made the peace offer and I accepted. Now I have the chance to work two shifts at the plant this summer. I have no other choice. Besides, Grandma Rose and you two have nothing to do with Grandma Rose and me. It's about time you got to know each other. She *is* your grandmother, after all. Anyway, having you kids this summer is her way of apologizing."

"For what?" Teddy dug deeper.

"Very simply this," her mother said. "When she *finally* honored us with her esteemed presence that time in Tacoma, she was only late by two years. I didn't need her in 1936. I needed her in 1934."

"Better late than never . . . ," Teddy mumbled.

Howie quietly socked her.

"Don't interrupt, Theadora. Oh, never mind. You wouldn't understand."

"I won't interrupt," Teddy said.

"It was right after Nah Nah Stokes died," Dee Dee continued, almost wistfully. She looked for the gas-station attendant, then honked impatiently.

"Nah Nah Stokes?" Teddy asked, unable to put a face on the name she'd never heard mentioned outside of anger. "Did you really call her Nah Nah?"

"I never called her anything. I was scared to death of my grandmother," Dee Dee replied, as though Teddy should have known that. "Anyway, Rose paid us that little surprise visit. She caught me off guard. I didn't have time to think. There she was, standing on the front steps like nothing was wrong between us. Like it was all hearts and roses. Then, after that . . . Oh, never mind, huh? That was eight years ago."

Dee Dee rescarfed her hair as she spoke, tucking here and poufing there. She added a final, "So relax, there's nothing to be scared of."

"I'm not scared!" Teddy shouted back at her mother. "You're the one who's scared! You haven't stopped primping for three whole weeks, Mom!"

"Why, you . . . !" Dee Dee growled, leaning over the seat to grab her daughter. Teddy pulled back, knowing the exact length of her mother's arm. "Well, all right, Miss Smarty Pants, maybe I am a little scared. Every girl should be scared of her mother."

It was Howie, peacemaker, who suspended the skirmish by saying, "Mom, your mascara's a little flaky."

Dee Dee kept a stern eye on Teddy, who smiled at her mother and said, "It's true, Mom. Like little bug tracks. Right there."

Dee Dee turned around to inspect the situation in the mirror and issued an "oh damn," while Teddy and Howie looked coolly at one another. Howie mouthed the words "leave her alone!" and Teddy returned his order with an obscene gesture.

The filling-station attendant, clearly born 4-F, finally arrived and, Coke-bottle glasses or not, gave Dee Dee the up and down, then asked, "Fill 'er up, lady?"

Dee Dee, never liking a man, any man (blind or not), to see her with smudged mascara, quickly put on her sunglasses and replied, "Yes. And check the oil, the water, the tires and the wipers, huh?" She smiled up at him demurely and asked, "Are your rest rooms clean?"

He pointed around to the side of the building and replied, "Hosed 'em down myself this morning."

Dee Dee once again turned around and asked Teddy, "You want to tidy up first?"

"Don't have to, Mom. You go ahead, though, I'll catch a coupla hours' sleep."

"If you think I'm going to let Grandma Rose's first glance of you be in those awful clothes, then you have another think coming, missy. Now, get out your suitcase. I want you to wear that yellow dress . . . the one with the sash. I bought you some new anklets. They're inside your Mary Janes. Howard, hand me my blue makeup case, will you, dear?"

"Mom! I'm not wearing that rotten yellow dress! I hate it! Look, Grandma Rose better get used to me looking just the way I am right now, 'cause that's the way I'm dressing!"

Dee Dee pursed her perfect lips and said petulantly, "Really, Theadora, I won't be seeing you all summer. You'd think doing this *one* little thing for me, so I can please my own mother, wouldn't be such a big deal. But that's okay. If you have no more pride in your appearance than those filthy dungarees, then fine. We'll let Rose think she has twin grandsons." She looked at Howard and added the finishing touch: "Howard dear, you'll be sure to put on a clean shirt and one of those clip-on ties for Grandma Rose, won't you, huh? Need a comb?" She rummaged through her purse and pulled out a comb, tugged off and tossed a mass of springy red hair, then handed it to Howard.

She got out of the car and added, "I'll only be a minute."

Teddy watched her mother disappear into the rest room, then glanced over to her brother as he got out of the car. She got out, met him at the trunk and watched him go through his suitcase for a clean shirt and a clip-on. Without looking at her, he simply said, "Hey, it's no skin off my nose changing shirts. This one's beginning to smell raunchy any-way." Then he sniffed the air, made a face and added, "Oh, or is that you?" And he left for the men's room.

Teddy looked down at her faded jeans, her men's extra-large sweatshirt and her walked-over saddle shoes and saw nothing wrong. Her mother exited the ladies' room, paused fetchingly to adjust the seams in her hose, then walked back to the car. Her perfume arrived before she did, and she smiled vaguely at her daughter as she plopped her blue makeup case into the trunk.

"Aw, Christ!" Teddy moaned, pulling her suitcase out of the trunk and hauling it to the ladies' room.

Several minutes later, the ladies' room door opened, and Teddy peeked around cautiously. The yellow dress, com-plete with sash, was several inches too small in all direc-tions except the bustline, making her feel like the giant anchor weight in a chorus line of toddlers. The patent leather Mary Janes, bought with last year's shoe ration coupons, were too tight, and the starched, lace-topped socks itched her ankles.

She heaved her suitcase into the trunk, slamming the top down so hard it rocked the car. She seized the back-door handle, plopped herself in, slammed the door shut, then glared at her brother with the intent to kill should he dare to draw so much as an uneven breath.

Howie put his hand to his face and looked out the window. He had suffered a run-in once before over the ill-sized yellow dress.

Dee Dee smiled victoriously at her daughter. She unsnapped her purse and handed Teddy a new pair of white gloves, saying, "Here, I got you these, Theadora. But don't put them on now, you'll only get them dirty. Aren't they lovely? I got them on sale at Woolworth's. See? The lace matches the lace on your anklets."

Teddy thought her teeth might crumble under the pressure of her jaw. "Mom, if you think I'm hiding these from Grandma Rose, you're crazy!" She held her scarred fingers up to her mother's face.

"Oh, don't be silly. It's only a first impression I'm concerned with. Now, do as I tell you, huh? Put them on just before we get there."

Teddy grabbed the gloves with a snap and placed them on the seat between herself and Howie. While her mother spoke, Teddy took the lid off of her fountain pen and placed the tip on the gloves. She watched the ink being absorbed deliciously into the creamy, lacy fabric, smiling at her own clever wickedness. Her eyes met Howie's, and she gave him her most vicious I-dare-you glare.

Once they were safely on Highway 101 south, Dee Dee said over her shoulder, "All right. Now, kids. Quiz. One last time, huh?"

Both Howie and Teddy let out a moan. "Aw, Mom, not the quiz again," Howie said.

"It's so stupid," Teddy added, opening and snapping shut the backseat ashtray.

"Come on, last time. Stop doing that, Theadora. Only the main issues this time. Okay, I'll be Grandma Rose and you be you." As she began the questions, just the main issues, she elevated her voice somewhat. "Tell me, children, how much money does your mother make?"

Together they answered, "Enough to get by."

"Oh, but it must be sooo hard, two children and no man. *How* do you all get by?"

"With love."

"Well, why is it your mother never remarried? Surely she must have had offers."

Teddy and Howie looked at each other. Holding in their twin smirks, they replied in singsong unison, "Oh yes, many, many offers. But *we* come first with Mother."

Dee Dee moved the mirror so that she could look directly at her children. She asked earnestly, "You won't say it like that, will you? It's true. You know it is."

"Mom, don't worry. If Grandma Rose asks, we'll tell her what you want us to," Howie said.

Dee Dee asked hopefully, "Honor Bright?"

Howie replied loyally, "Honor Bright."

Dee Dee readjusted the mirror and added, "Just remember, your grandmother can be very tricky. She lays traps."

Teddy leaned forward and asked, "What if I slip up and tell her the truth? What if she drags it out of me if she's so tricky?"

Teddy watched her mother's dimples grow deeper as she clenched her jaw in anger. "All right, Theadora, you tell me what you think the truth is."

Teddy paused, knowing full well she had the power to set her mother off into a flying tirade that could, considering the tourist traffic on Highway 101, kill them all. So she opted for the truth laced with righteousness. "Okay, since you insist, I think the truth is we're dirt poor, always have been, always will be, and no thanks to ol' Rose, who probably has lots of money and never sends us one red dime. There, is that the truth?" Teddy didn't take her eyes off the rearview mirror as her mother considered her reply.

"Mom?" Teddy finally asked, touching her mother's shoulder. With a closer look into the mirror, Teddy could see tears slipping delicately into her mother's dimples. "You mad? I didn't mean to make you cry," Teddy said helplessly, looking at Howie.

"You okay, Mom?" Howie asked, leaning forward and reaching out to her. Dee Dee tried to smile, grasped Howie's hand and gripped it for support. Teddy sat back down.

"I'm sorry, Mom, but you asked. I'm sorry." She looked out the window, trying to figure out what there was to cry about. It had never much bothered her that they were always broke. Howie never seemed to mind. Why should their mom?

"Just promise Mom you'll tell Rose what we practiced," Howie prompted.

"I promise," Teddy said.

"Honor Bright?" Howie asked.

"Yeah, yeah."

THREE

An hour later, Dee Dee slowed the Plymouth down, from thirty to fifteen, signaled and took a right-hand turnoff from 101 into the town of Holiday Beach, Oregon.

"Here, Howard, tell me where to turn," Dee Dee said, handing her son the directions.

"The town has five whole houses, Mother, how hard can it be?" Teddy grumbled, looking around at the tall, wind-torn pines that hid the sparsely planted beach cabins.

"'Left on Seaview,'" Howard read importantly. "'Then right on Pacific. Six blocks. Last house on left. Three stories with a widow's walk.' Whatever that is."

Dee Dee brought the car to a humble, hesitant crawl as they approached the last house on the left. Nearly hidden by the pines, it peered cautiously down at them. It was a monstrosity encased in weathered gray shakes and laced with countless French-paned windows with green sashes. Like an ancient mariner's wedding cake, it was topped with the widow's walk, complete with telescope.

19

Teddy craned her neck to take in all three stories. "Not bad for an old widow," she mumbled to Howie.

"Ready for D day?" Howie whispered back.

"You mean Dee-Dee day," Teddy replied, looking at their mother primping nervously in the front seat.

Dee Dee turned around, her face solemn, pale, serious. "Well, I guess we're here. How's my face?"

A refreshing coastal breeze tinted with the scent of dormant beach bonfires greeted Teddy as she got out of the car. She noticed how much cooler the air was.

All three car doors slammed simultaneously as the trio waited for someone, presumably Grandma Rose, to greet them. Dee Dee looked at her children with dainty but measured apprehension.

Howard walked to his mother, took her hand and asked, "You okay, Mom?"

Teddy noticed how much larger the threatening tears made her mother's eyes appear. She dutifully stepped up and took her mother's other hand, which was cold and shaking.

"Wanna turn back, Mom?" she whispered.

Dee Dee shook off her children's hands and said, "You're going to fight me right up to the last minute, aren't you, Theadora? Where are your gloves?"

Teddy knew better than to apologize. She simply answered through gritted teeth, "I got ink on them. Mom, I don't want to be here. . . ."

"I told you, I'm not thrilled with it either! What do you mean, you got ink on them?"

"Mom, quick, let's go home."

20

"Nonsense! I didn't hoard gas coupons for six months just to turn tail and run." Then, with a pointed finger from her own gloved hand, Dee Dee added, "And you and me are going to settle up on that glove account, missy! Seventy cents, I'll have you know!"

Then Dee Dee leaned through the car window and gave the horn two solid, short toots. Those two innocent toots rang out like a death knell to Teddy. *That's it. The alarm has sounded. Nowhere to run. Nowhere to hide.*

They looked up. The house appeared to be cool, vacant of both welcome and resident. A reprieve? The only sound was a seagull far above.

"You sure she's expecting us?" Teddy asked her mother.

"I wrote and told her we'd be arriving late on Friday, the ninth of June." Dee Dee looked again at the huge house and called out a long, melodic "Yooo-hooo!" No answer, so she said, "Well, guess we better find the front door."

Just as they were walking around the ivy-crested walkway, a woman called down from a second-story window. "Delores? Is that you?"

Dee Dee froze at the sound of her mother's voice. She tried to call out "Yes," but her voice was weak. She cleared her throat, then tried once more. "We're down here . . . Mama."

Dee Dee whirled around and faced her children. Teddy noticed how her fingers were shaking as she adjusted the straps of her sundress. She asked, "Are my seams straight?"

And Howie replied, "You look terrific, Mom."

Teddy's hands instinctively dug into her for-show-only pockets. She heard a screen door slam, followed by heels on the walkway. Then Grandma Rose appeared, stopping

21

short as she beheld her daughter. Teddy wasn't sure what to expect. She wondered if they'd fall into each other's arms, tearful apologies filling in the gaping canyon their separation had formed. Or maybe a cautious standoff . . . a cool "So how ya been?"

Dee Dee simply said, "Mama?"

As though there could be any doubt—they were as alike as bookends holding in eight years of *Vogue* magazines. Pretty white face, deep dimples, startling blue eyes, wavy red hair, tall, slender. *Rose must have been just a teenager when she had my mother,* Teddy thought. *Like mother, like daughter . . . oh God, is that the way it's really going to be?*

Rose walked to her daughter, smiled warmly, beheld her double and said, "Oh, Delores." She offered an embrace, which Dee Dee awkwardly returned. Then they stood back, held hands and told each other how terrific they looked.

"And the twins," gushed Rose. "How could we have been apart so long? Why, they're practically all grown up." She paused to examine them side by side. "And, yes, you can really tell they're twins."

Teddy and Howie were twinly insulted, but they each planted a dutiful kiss on their grandmother's cool, powdered cheek and tried to smile in the agonizing moment.

"Well, let's not stand out here for God to gawk at. Come on inside. I have a big vat of chili cooking. Beer and chili. Remember how often we used to have that, Dee Dee?" Rose put her arm around Dee Dee's waist, but Dee Dee broke away and handed the car keys to Howie, saying, "Bring in a load, huh, kids?"

Teddy watched as Rose and Dee Dee walked up the path, side by side yet curiously distant.

"Well? What do you think?" Howie asked as he pulled luggage out from the trunk.

Teddy picked up a rock and heaved it down the dirt road. "Hell, just my luck. The only bright part of being stuck here this whole summer was being rid of Mom. But look at her. Grandma Rose is every ounce of fluff Mom is."

"Well, at least we know where she gets it," Howie said. "Say, but dig this place. It's huge! We might do all right for ourselves here. Might be able to work for the old lady. Cash is cash." Loaded with luggage, he turned and yelled at his sister. "Hey, you gonna just stand there getting uglier or you gonna help with this crap?"

Teddy pulled out the remainder of the luggage and was quick to inform her brother that she was able to carry half again as much as he was . . . in a dress and last year's Mary Janes, no less.

"Yeah, you're one helluva guy," Howie growled as he led the way up the steps, only to be overtaken by Teddy and shoved aside.

The main entrance was around the front of the house, which faced the Pacific Ocean. The view was incredible. Out front, huge rocks erupted out of the surf, promising daring low-tide exploration. To the north, high green hills tumbled toward the ocean, then dropped off suddenly, as though a sea monster had taken a huge bite out of them.

Teddy and Howie paused to take in their summer view. From the car below, a persistent, spoiled yapping ruined the serenity.

Howard turned to his sister and said, "You better go get Perkie. She might roast in that car."

"So?" Teddy asked back.

"Fine," Howie said, opening the screen door. "All you need is Mom blaming you for that dog biting the dust."

"It's *her* dog. *She* went off and left her," Teddy defended herself. "Why don't *you* go down and get her?"

Howie set down a suitcase, slapped the car keys into her hand and stared at his sister, replying cruelly, "Because I'm older and you're the one who needs to build Brownie points with Mom. And if that's not enough, I'll tell Mom you inked those gloves on purpose!"

Teddy threw her load of luggage down at Howie's legs, recognizing a hopeless cause when she saw one. "All right, but you haul that junk in!"

She started back down the walkway, and Howie called after her, "I hope Perkie bites your ugly face off!"

So grateful was Perkie to be released from the hot car that, for once, she didn't try to take a bite out of Teddy. Teddy attached the rhinestone leash and encouraged the dog to follow her back up the steps. But it was sniff, pee, pant, pant, pee, sniff before the Pekingese finally complied.

Teddy opened the screen door, then stood there, feeling the evening breeze rush through, bringing with it the smell of chili and cigarette smoke. Perkie strolled royally in, and Teddy, paralyzed, simply dropped the leash. She had second thoughts and the keys to the car. How far could she get before anyone noticed she was gone? Normandy, France, probably.

Then she heard her mother's voice gush, "Oh look, here comes my widdle Perkie-Werkie. How'd you get in here?" This was followed by some undecipherable goo-gooing as Perkie conquered her new territory.

Teddy couldn't face the front room, Dee Dee, her grandmother and Perkie just yet. She gently closed the screen door and went back around the house, careful to stay away from the front-room windows. Instead, she peeked through the lower windows as she explored the perimeter of the house. A wing, no doubt added as an afterthought, seemed to have a service entrance. She tried the door, and it opened. She slipped inside and was immediately greeted with the cool, moldy odors of ancient things . . . fraying tennis shoes caked with sand, a row of rubber boots standing at attention in escalating sizes, an old wringer washer with sandy overalls draped over the tub, rusty clam shovels, and canvas cots and tents hanging from the rafters like giant, mold-spotted bats. Odd accessories, thought Teddy, for the Rose she'd just met. In a corner she recognized the patriotic piles of newspapers, tin cans, and a gallon of used kitchen fat—everywhere on earth, Teddy thought, reminders of war.

Through the vents in the ancient coal furnace she could hear the muted voices of her family somewhere up and to the left. It really wasn't illegal entry, Teddy told herself. She was a guest in her grandmother's home, simply exploring. She took the staircase up, assuming she'd come out in a kitchen or pantry. Instead, the door opened into a hallway. She went down the hall, away from the sounds of her family, and found herself faced with the choice of two doors.

Closet, she assumed, as she quietly opened one door. To her pleasant surprise, she found still another set of stairs. Only these were tightly enclosed in the staircase, the steps many and steep. Closing the door behind her, she took the steps, carefully walking on the outsides, keeping the tattle-tale creaking to a minimum.

There was a wide door at the top. She gave it a shove, and it opened with a gush of warm, stale attic air. She knew, the minute she stepped in, she'd found the perfect refuge for the summer. It was dark, airy, mysterious, yet oddly comforting and welcoming. And there, to the right, yet another hatch at the top of a three-step ladder.

She ventured higher still. The widow's walk? Perfect! She could tell it'd been some time since the hatch had been freed of its latch. She shoved it open with a determined push. She carefully pulled herself up, cursing the yellow dress and grinning wickedly at the sound of the sash ripping on a nail.

The widow's walk. It was merely a platform, six by six perhaps, just enough room for the skirts of a sea captain's wife to rustle upon as she paced, aching with gray loneliness or perhaps blushing with scarlet betrayal. How long did a wife have to wait until the sea captain was presumed dead?

The walk had a rickety fence holding in the edges, but it seemed to be for nothing more than decoration. . . . A person could easily fall and call it a day. Ah yes, that must have been what the properly grieving widow was supposed to do in the old days . . . cast herself from the rooftop.

The old brass telescope was green with age, spotted white with seagull droppings, and its swivel stand was anchored tight with rust. Teddy looked through the telescope, and although the view was foggy and vague, the lens was still intact. The telescope was permanently trained on a stream that ran next to the house, sparkling in welcome as it wound its lazy way to the ocean.

Too bad she wasn't a kid anymore, Teddy thought as she took in the potentials—the logs, the rocks, the grasses. What adventure, what fantasy, what explorations could be had in such a place! Yes, too bad she wasn't a kid.

FOUR

The thrill of Teddy's discoveries was brought to an abrupt end when she heard the shrill voice of her mother calling from below: "TheeeeeaDOOOOORRRRRaaaaaa?"

Not answering would only make her come looking, so Teddy called back, "Right there, Mom!" She was sure she couldn't be seen high above the third-story dormers.

"Where *are* you?" Dee Dee called out in a general upward direction. "You better not be climbing trees in that dress!"

Kneeling behind the fence, she called back down, "No, Mom."

She latched the door tight behind her and scrambled down the attic stairs. Taking only one wrong turn, she ended up back in the basement. She ran through the laundry area, out the door and back up the walkway. When she finally appeared in the front room, she was flushed from the sprint. Cobwebs had caught on her hair and shoulders, and of course, the yellow dress was now delightfully torn and hanging pitifully around her hairy legs. A fruitful exploration indeed.

Teddy glanced quickly around the room: knotty pine paneling, aged to a warm perfection; a magnificent stone fireplace; deep, welcoming chairs; a staircase spilling up; bay windows spilling out.

Howie, who was sitting in a grand high-back wing chair while sipping a cola from a straw, looked at her with a suspicious eye. It was obvious she'd been having more fun than he.

Dee Dee stood up.

"Theadora! Look at you! What have you managed to get yourself into?" Dee Dee demanded. She examined the torn hem and whisked the dust off Teddy's shoulders.

"I was, a . . . cleaning out the backseat of the car," Teddy replied, issuing the lie with not so much as a twinge of guilt.

Rose came over to her and handed her a cool cola, and as Teddy reached for it, Rose noticed her hands. If she was startled at first, her recovery was swift. "Oh, I'd forgotten. . . . Tell me, dear, do your hands ever bother you?"

The room was stone silent. Dee Dee rushed to explain. "Theadora has gotten quite—"

"Yes, darling, but I was asking her," Rose cut in.

Teddy looked at her mother with a faint air of apprehension as she replied, "It only bothers me that they bother some people."

Rose smiled warmly at her and replied, "Good for you, Theadora."

"Oh, but you ought to hear Theadora play the piano, Mother. I taught her. Really, she plays just fine," Dee Dee offered.

"I don't either, Mom, I play like sh—" Teddy caught her

mother's eye, then finished, "Chopin. Just like him. Can't tell us apart."

"You were right the first time," Howie grumbled through his straw.

"Well, then maybe later you'll play for us?" Rose asked. "But now, wouldn't you like to change before dinner, dear?"

"Boy, would I," Teddy replied, remembering the familiar refuge of her jeans and sweatshirt, wadded up and waiting in her suitcase.

"Go put on that blue dress, Theadora. You know, the daisy print one," Dee Dee suggested, crossing to the fireplace mantel and taking a cigarette out of a case. She took a match, struck it along the rockery of the fireplace and added between inhalations, "It's in your red suitcase."

"I didn't have room for my books, so I took it out," Teddy replied. Books were usually a safe lie.

"Well, Theadora," Dee Dee said, her long fingers holding her cigarette with a movie star's sophistication. She gave her daughter a hopeless frown and added, "Well, then I guess you'll just have to put on your plaid skirt and green sweater."

Teddy raised her eyebrows, making Dee Dee add, "You *did* pack your plaid skirt and green sweater, didn't you?"

"I brought a lot of books, Mom," Teddy replied.

"Darn you, Theadora," Dee Dee went on, blowing out smoke dramatically, "I work so hard for all your lovely clothes. I wanted you to—"

But it was Rose this time who spoke, just as Teddy was beginning to take aim. "Oh, why all the formality? This is the beach for God's sake, and we're not exactly having a seven-course dinner. Just chili and beer. First impressions are over. We all passed. Now, go change into something comfortable, Theadora. You too, Howard. Delores, wouldn't you like to change? I will if you will."

"No thank you, Mother. I'm quite comfortable, thank you."

"Mom?" Howie asked, holding his tie up hopefully.

"Oh, all right, go change," Dee Dee said, grinding out her cigarette with resignation.

Howie jumped up and led Teddy to the staircase. By habit, they raced up the stairs.

"My room looks out at those huge rocks," Howie bragged, pointing at the seagulled monolith erupting from the shore outside.

"So, what'd you think?" Teddy asked, barely giving the view a half glance.

Howie carefully disconnected his clip-on tie, then unbuttoned his dress shirt while he answered, "I think they're neat. I wonder if we can climb 'em."

"Not those rocks! About her! Rose, you dope!"

"Hey, where the heck did you go, by the way? Cleaning out the car, my foot!"

"Exploring," Teddy said, taking his discarded tie and clicking the clamps back and forth.

Howie snatched it from her and said, "You were snooping."

"Shut up," she returned flatly, now going through the top dresser drawer. "So, what'd you think?"

Howie caught Teddy's reflection in the mirror and asked, "About Rose? I don't know. She's all right, I guess. A lot younger than I thought she'd be. What'd you think?"

"I think Mom's head ought to be examined for getting us into this," Teddy answered, walking toward the door. "Probably Rose's too."

"*Your* head ought to be examined," Howie said, reaching into his suitcase for a change of clothes.

"Go to hell," Teddy retorted as she slammed the door on her brother. She found her luggage in the room across the hall. A room with no view of the ocean, but with a large bathroom attached and a window that overlooked the stream to the north.

She quickly changed. She and Howie emerged at the same time. They were dressed nearly identically—in brown cords and blue sweatshirts.

"Hey, Howie," Teddy began, stopping at the top of the stairs. "Remember our promise?"

Howie paused and stared at his sister. "Yeah. So what about it?"

"Nothing. Just wanted to make sure you remembered it."

"Well, you *know* Rose is going to ask about the fire, sooner or later."

"I'm telling you, the minute she does, I'm long gone."

"So what're you gonna do? Join the marines or hop a freighter?" Howie asked sarcastically.

He started down the steps, but Teddy pulled him back by his sleeve. Her face was hard and serious, her eyes focused and urgent. "I mean it, Howie. We promised not to talk about it. Ever. Not to Rose or anyone."

"What's with you?"

"Mom said Rose can be tricky. If she asks, just tell her you don't remember," Teddy whispered.

"But I don't remember, Teddy," Howie replied quietly, honestly. "You know that."

"Tell you what, Rose gets snoopy about that Christmas, just tell her 'Teddy might remember,' but you don't. Got it?"

Howie's face softened, and for a moment, the twins' faces were identical. "Roger," he whispered back.

"I want more than 'Roger.' I want 'Honor Bright,' " Teddy whispered, still holding on to his sleeve.

"I don't see what the big deal is." But her eyes were locked on his, and he added, "All right. Honor Bright."

With that, she released him, and he continued down the stairs.

Teddy went back into her room, changed into a gray sweatshirt, then rejoined the rest of her family downstairs.

FIVE

The dining room was glowing with the glory of the sunset over the Pacific. Large bay windows on two sides allowed a magnificent view of the rocks, the ocean and the mysterious fog bank above.

"When I moved down here, I had to cover up all these wonderful windows with that horrible black cloth. I tell you, it was like a funeral parlor in this house. Weren't those early war days awful, Dee Dee?" Rose asked, filling her daughter's mug with beer from a pitcher.

"Well, up our way, what with Boeing and the shipyards and of course Fort Lewis, well, for a while, we all just knew we were going to be bombed to kingdom come. But the blackouts never bothered me much. They scared Howie, but Teddy loved them." She looked around the room, as though counting the windows, then added, "You must have four times more windows than I do."

"Want me to count them?" Teddy asked, one step away from sarcasm and thin ice.

Dee Dee ignored her and continued, "Actually, it's the

rationing that drives me nuts. Now, I ask you, what's so rational about rationing? I mean, it's not as though nylons and sugar and decent dress material aren't available. All you have to do is know the right people and have the bucks and you can get anything on the black market—"

"You better also have a good lawyer if you get caught," Rose interjected.

"So," Dee Dee continued with a wistful sigh, "I'm stuck taking a filthy old bus to work all summer, just to hoard enough gas coupons to get back down here in August." She took a long sip of beer. She fanned her mouth and added, "Gawd, Mother, spicy chili."

"Don't you remember? I always made it spicy."

Teddy and Howie exchanged glances. They both knew spice had nothing to do with any heat around the table that night.

"What was I saying?" Dee Dee asked. "Oh yes, rationing. Really, if this war was being run by women, rationing would be a thing of the past. I mean if Eleanor Roosevelt cared a little more about how she looked, I have no doubt that she'd make sure we could get a decent pair of nylons, for crissakes."

"If this war was being run by women, there wouldn't be a war," Rose said, taking a long drink.

"Well, that's a mute point."

"Moot," Rose corrected.

Dee Dee glared at her mother and took another drink of beer.

Teddy kept a half eye on her mother and grandmother as they ate chili, drank beer and gently began to spar. How alike they looked, right down to the nail polish. Was there some evil family flaw that forced the women into frivolous outer wrappings? Was there some gene passed on from generation to generation that demanded paint, polish, straight seams? Oh God, was it in the genes? Was the same fate awaiting her some hideous day when the dreaded hormones finished their devastating handiwork?

On the brighter side, a special "welcome" cake was presented for dessert, a creamy white affair with ruby red scrolling. "For My Family," it warned.

"I borrowed so much sugar for this, my neighbors must think I'm hoarding," Rose confessed. She passed around generous, gooey slices and refilled the beer pitcher.

As the world outside drew darker, the world inside grew lighter, smokier, and the careful reminiscing grew louder . . . all easy stuff at first . . . childhood highlights mostly. The two women skirted the perimeters of their lives with and without each other. Caution. Such caution.

To Teddy's relief, she and her brother were given a timely dismissal when Nah Nah Stokes was mentioned. The twins were shown the radio in the library, and there they sat, amid the mahogany, listening to the fuzzy AMs, abandoning the impossible FMs, browsing through the rows and rows of dusty volumes, eavesdropping on the conversation drifting their way from the dining room.

"Think things'll get hot?" Howie asked, looking down the hall, his face an amalgam of concern and curiosity.

"Of course it'll get hot, you dope!" Teddy replied, climbing a library ladder and trying to ascertain what sort of person her grandmother was by the literary company she kept.

"Two bits says we're out of here by midnight," Howie said after a particularly loud retort came from the dining room.

"Wishful thinking," Teddy muttered to the volumes before her.

"Think they'll get drunk and have it all out?" Howie asked.

Teddy shrugged and said, "Probably."

"Mom shouldn't drink at times like this," Howie continued.

"Want to know what I think? I think Mom's just jealous of Rose's money," Teddy said, pulling out and blowing on an old book. "Hey, look at this: *A Tale of Two Cities*! It's ancient! I'll bet it's valuable and it's just sitting here, rotting."

"Shhh," Howie warned, leaning closer into the dining-room conversation. Teddy climbed down and joined her brother, holding the book close to her heart. Howie looked at the book, noticed his sister was shaking. "You cold?" he asked.

"Yeah. Shut up. What're they talking about?"

"Something about men."

"Figures." She leaned into the opposite side of the threshold, paging through the precious book, attempting an I-don't-give-a-damn posture. But she looked up, closed the book and took a deep, calming breath when the words got louder.

"Well, you were wrong, Mama! You don't know how awful it was! You weren't there, for God's sake!"

"It's not as though I could have *done* anything!" Rose screamed back. "Besides, I've told you and told you and told you, I couldn't come! I wanted to, but I had Nah Nah to take care of! She was dying!"

"The hell she was! That old hag lived two more years!"

"I couldn't leave her, Dee Dee!"

"You wouldn't leave her, Mama! You goddamned wouldn't leave her!" Dee Dee cried back. "You chose that awful old woman—the one you always swore you hated—over—over *me*! Your own daughter!"

"I tell you, I couldn't . . . ," Rose repeated, this time weaker, wearier.

"What'd she do, put a spell on you? Huh, Mama? Didn't you tell her I needed you?"

"You wouldn't understand, Dee Dee."

"Tell me, Mama, does it bother you that you don't have the same power over me that your mother had over you, huh?" Dee Dee asked, a smear of superiority in her voice.

Teddy'd heard enough. Without saying anything, she walked down the hall toward the dining room, making sure her footsteps could be heard. The women looked up and stopped talking as Teddy entered.

Dee Dee, eyes large, face dully pink, said, "Oh, Theadora." She took a slug of beer, recouped and asked, "Say, would you take poor liddle Perkie out? She has to gogetum. Her leash is next to the door."

"Why can't Howie? He's just sitting around doing nothing. I'm going to bed. Rose, I found this book in the library. It looks really old. Probably worth something. Can I read it?"

A brilliant tactic of avoidance: asking permission to read

a classic instead of standing around, encouraging a spiteful Pekingese at the end of a rhinestone leash to gogetum.

"It's pretty depressing," Rose commented, standing up with a slight sway.

"Then she'll love it," Dee Dee remarked blandly.

"Tell you what, you can have that old book, Teddy. Come on, Delores, let's you and me go walk the dog. Fresh air'll do us both good, and we're too drunk to go playing around anymore in the past."

"Oh no, Theadora can walk Perkie," Dee Dee objected with a swish of her hand.

"Mother, I'm really tired," Teddy moaned, testing the waters and wondering if her new ally would intercede again.

"See? You go to bed, Teddy," Rose insisted. "I promise, we'll keep it quiet down here."

Without looking at her mother, Teddy started to leave.

"Theadora!" Dee Dee shouted.

Teddy stopped and demanded, "What?"

"I'm not talking to you," Dee Dee snapped, staring at her mother.

"Me? What?" Rose asked innocently.

"Her name is TheaDORa," Dee Dee replied. "If I wanted her to be called Teddy, I'd have named her Teddy!"

"Oh, don't be so touchy. Teddy's a darling name. You've never complained about being called Dee Dee." A smirk covered Rose's fading lipstick.

"I've always detested Dee Dee, now that you ask."

"I wasn't asking. Oh, go on up to bed, The-a-DOR-a," Rose said. "De-LOR-es and Rose-MAR-y will walk Gogetum or whatever the blazes that beast's name is."

There was no way Teddy was going to offer her cheek for

beerish, lipstick-stained kisses, so she offered a cool good night. *A Tale of Two Cities* her breastplate, she backed out of the room.

Teddy walked past her brother in the hallway, and as she passed him, he pulled her back and whispered, "Well?"

"Well what?"

"They getting along or what?"

"Who cares? I got what I wanted," Teddy replied, showing him the book and leaving.

She slammed her bedroom door, hid Dickens, wrote in her journal, then lay awake until 2 A.M.

SIX

JE119—*The room's okay; blue, not yellow, thank God. I think this Grandma Rose person is loaded. Rich, I mean. Everything in this room is new . . . even the junk on the dressing table. As though I'd ever actually use that stuff. Nail polish—what a joke! Putting nail polish on these hands is like putting cologne on a shitwagon.*

They're still downstairs, Mom and Rose. I can hear them through the furnace grate. It all goes back to the accident, the fire. I knew it would. Rose wasn't around. So big deal if Mom needed her. Mom's so stupid. She can't even see she's ditching me now just like Rose ditched her back then. Just goes to show, you end up with just yourself. So I don't know why Mom gets so worked up about it. Past is past. I think I heard Mom mention Francesca. Oh please God, don't let her start talking about Francesca. Please, please, please. Oh, stop worrying, you nitwit. Mom's drunk. She'll forget anyway. Howie and me promised. Maybe we should have made Mom promise too. We should have done it. Made her pledge her own

41

damn Honor Bright before we even pulled out of the drive-way. I don't want to hear any more. There! I put some books over the grate. God, my head's killing me. Times like this I wish I'd never been born.

The next morning, Saturday, over breakfast, Dee Dee announced to her children she'd decided to return home that morning, rather than waiting until Sunday as she had originally planned.

"But why, Mom?" Howie asked. His mouth stopped chewing as he looked across the table at her.

"Because if I get started today, I won't have to miss work Monday," she explained as Rose poured her another cup of coffee. "Thank you, Mother."

Teddy examined their faces: eyes puffy, skin blotchy, noses stuffy. Hair, makeup perfect. Hands shaky. *Too many tears or too many beers?* she wondered, before reminding herself she didn't care.

"Gee, Mom," Howie asked, "do you think that's wise? Sunday traffic and all?"

"Oh, sweetheart, I'll be all right," Dee Dee said, touching his hand softly.

"Well, Delores," Rose began, adding a fresh stack of pancakes to the serving platter, "I wish you could stay longer. It seems like we just started catching up. So many years to make up for. It's a shame, really."

"I wish I could stay too," Dee Dee replied formally, "but this is war. Somebody has to build those ships."

Then it occurred to Teddy as she examined their faces: either the two women had no recollection whatsoever of the previous night, or they were going to play the game through to a stalemate and act as though there was nothing more disagreeable between them, in the clear light of sober day, than which hue of shampoo tint to use.

As though Rose heard Teddy's silent summation, she turned to Dee Dee and said kindly, "Yes, this awful war, keeping families apart. There ought to be a law. But I know you have to go, dear. You're only doing your part. Maybe by having the twins here with me this summer, I'll be doing a little something for the war too. Besides, we can catch up in August. When we have more time together. You will plan on staying down longer, won't you?"

What a shovelful, Teddy thought as she bit her tongue and forced down some orange juice.

"I'll try. Well, I won't be able to thank you enough, Mother," Dee Dee said, daintily patting her lips with her napkin. "For having the kids, I mean." She lit a cigarette, blew the smoke out over the table and added, "I dread that awful car trip home, especially without the kids to help me out." She popped Perkie a piece of pancake and spoke, lips pursed, to the dog. "Well, my liddle Perkie will help her mommy, won't she?"

"Now? Right now, you're leaving?" Howie asked, his face going a little pale.

Dee Dee rose and fixed her son's collar as she passed his chair. "Finish your breakfast. I'm just going to load my bag into the car."

Teddy looked up and found that Rose was smiling kindly down at her. As their eyes met, Rose quickly said to Dee Dee, "Need any help, dear?"

"No thanks, but you know what I do need? Theadora, would you mind walking Perkie for me, huh? You're finished, aren't you? Thanks." She handed Teddy the leash and left to gather her things. Rose followed her out of the kitchen.

"You do it," Teddy ordered, handing Howie the leash. She scowled down at the dog, who was begging at her feet, panting little snorts.

"I'm still eating," Howie said, his face full of pancakes.

"Come on, you!" she grumbled, pulling the dog along to the front door, thinking how nice it would be to accidentally arrange for the dog to get squashed between the heavy door and the screen. What a great doorstop the beast would make, stuffed with iron and bronzed. What a keen going-away present for Mom. One Pekingese, incredibly dead.

"Now, Mother, I gave the children some spending money, so you're not to give them a penny more unless they do chores. Understood?" Dee Dee stood, hands gloved, purse in hand, sunglasses cunningly propped on her head. The car was warmed up and running.

"Understood," Rose repeated.

"Well, then I guess this is it," Dee Dee continued. There was a pause. She stood in front of Howie, took him in her arms, hugged him, then kissed him goodbye. Teddy made a note to tease him later about the tear she caught slipping out of his eye.

She was next. A cool hug, a faint kiss and a "Be a good girl, Theodora. Now watch your mouth." She released her, then added, "You too, Howard. No swearing. Honor Bright?"

"Sure, Mom."

"Theadora? Honor Bright?"

The two words always stuck in her craw, like admitting defeat, crying uncle. But she managed a weak "Honor Bright." Her hands were deep in her pockets, fingers crossed, safe at least in the thought that it would be her last Honor Bright until August.

Dee Dee was then face-to-face with her mother. Eye-to-eye, smile-to-smile. They embraced, and Teddy supposed, someone watching (not knowing the statistics) might think it was a fond and loving goodbye. She figured their fingers were crossed somewhere too.

Dee Dee situated her dog on its throne, then smiled out the driver's window at her family. She pulled her sunglasses down and blew a kiss as she attempted to start the engine. Already running, it growled angrily back at her, and she giggled weakly.

"Oops. Well, see you all in August," she said, clunking the car into gear.

"Call us when you get home," Howie reminded her.

They waved goodbye to the Plymouth as it pulled away, the thick tires spitting back a thin layer of sand.

Rose stood next to the twins, watching her daughter drive away. Teddy tried to read her expression . . . relief, regret or resignation?

Then Rose said, smiling faintly, "Well, I'd say that went pretty well, under the circumstances. What'd you think?"

Howie and Teddy looked at each other, aghast. That question wasn't on the quiz.

"Uh . . . y-yeah, Grandma," Howie stammered.

"Hold it. Let's get something straight right here and now,

buster," Rose interrupted sternly. "Anyone here calls me Grandma, and I'll have their liver for breakfast. That clear?"

Howie took an instinctive step closer to his sister. What the hell was going on? "Sure," he corrected himself, "Rose."

"Teddy?" Rose asked. "You want to keep your liver this summer?"

"Yeah, I might need it someday," she said carefully.

"Good. Step one. Now then," Rose asked Howie, "you did what I told you?"

"Yes."

"What?" Teddy asked. "Did what?"

"Rose had me hide a hundred bucks and three pair of silk stockings in Mom's purse," Howie replied. "A hundred bucks and real silk!"

"Why'd you have to hide it?"

"Because, stupid," Howie explained, his voice cracking a little, "you know Mom's too proud to just *take* it."

"Okay now, don't you two start," Rose said, gently pulling Howie away from his sister. "I wanted it to be a gift, and all gifts, I think, should be . . . you know . . . anonymous."

"Well, she'll know it was from you," Teddy said flatly, logically.

"Of course, she will," Rose agreed. Then she asked Howie, "Do you think she remembered everything? Her makeup case? That disgusting little dog's leash?"

Howie nodded, then sniffed.

"Good," Rose continued, slipping out of her high heels

and wiping her lipstick off with a tissue. "Then synchronize your watches: summer has officially begun."

"What d' you mean?" Teddy asked, watching her grandmother unscrew her earrings.

"I mean, sweet darling, I'm going upstairs to change." She then tugged at her perfectly coiffed hair until the wig came off. She tousled her thick salt-and-pepper hair (bobbed short and pageboyed) while Howie and Teddy stared unbelievingly.

Rose started up the walkway, barefoot, carrying the red wig and her shoes. She turned and looked down at her grandchildren and added, "You don't actually think I dress like *this*, do you?"

She practically ran up the walk and disappeared around the corner of the house. Howie's mouth was wide open. He looked at his sister for her explanation. "What the hell?" he managed. "What do you make of that?"

Teddy smiled, somehow intrigued. "I think I know where Rose's been all these years," she whispered.

"Where?" Howie whispered back.

"The nut house."

Howie's eyebrows hit his hairline as he asked seriously, "You think?"

"What do *you* think?" Teddy asked back, trying not to laugh at her brother's horrified expression.

Howie caught on, then said, "I think you're full of it."

"Oh yeah? Ever hear of a split personality? Maybe that's what Rose has," Teddy teased further, her voice low and mysterious. "Maybe she's a schizo. Mom probably did it to her."

"Get serious."

"And maybe," Teddy added, giving her throat an invisible slit, "that's what Rose is going to do to us—split *our* personalities." She began up the walk, turned and added wickedly, "Think about it."

SEVEN

The first hour after their mother's departure was the most awkward. Not sure where to go, what to do or say, Teddy and Howie simply sat in the living room, paging through magazines and keeping the talk light, insulting and simple. Since Rose had disappeared upstairs, presumably to change, there was little else to do except await her reemergence and decide whether Teddy's premonition of grand-infanticide would come true. Neither residents nor guests, they appeared more like young camp recruits, awaiting their cabin counselor to orchestrate their first day.

The Rose who appeared before them was 180 degrees away from the Rose who had first presented herself. Hair now free of wig; nails now free of polish; face now free of powder, rouge, and liner; and body now free of any garment even remotely suggesting restraint. She was oddly younger now in appearance. Rose certainly appeared more relaxed, and oddest of all, Teddy noticed an immediate resemblance between herself and her grandmother. Rose carried a round hatbox, which she set down next to her on the last step.

"Bored already?" Rose asked as she rolled her pants legs up.

Howie popped up and replied, "No, Rose. Uh, say, you look . . . good. You look good. And we were just wondering . . ."

"Yes?"

"Uh, where have you been living lately?" Howie pressed on courageously. "I mean, have you been living here long?"

"About nine years."

"Where before that?"

"Minneapolis. Why?"

"Oh, no reason. Just wondering."

"Howie thinks you have a split personality," Teddy offered simply.

"What?"

Howie gasped, "I don't either! *You* do!"

Rose laughed and said, "Only when I'm around your mother." Then, as if to back up her statement, she opened the hatbox, extracted the wig and shook it in front of the twins. "Look—this is the unreal Rose." She twirled around, then added, "And this is the real Rose. Now come on, you two. There's lots to catch up on." She left for the kitchen, putting an end to the Jekyll-Hyde issue.

Teddy followed, and as she passed Howie, he growled, "Creep!"

"Moron," she growled back.

The first item on Rose's agenda of the "officially begun" summer was showing the kids the large brass bell outside the kitchen door. She clanged it soundly and instructed them that when it rang, they were to hotfoot it home, no questions asked.

Do's and don'ts finally led to the last item: assigning Teddy and Howie chores in exchange for a very liberal allowance. Teddy cautiously agreed but silently assumed that this generosity was supposed to compensate for something lacking, such as Rose's presence in their lives. Guilt, no doubt. Money erased guilt in Teddy's mind; why else would judges assess fines? *Fifty cents wash, fifty cents dry . . . hell,* Teddy thought, *it's worth dirtying extra dishes just to fill the dishpan again. No telling what sweeping the walkway, beating the rugs or cleaning the attic might bring. Oooo . . . cleaning the attic . . .*

"You know, Rose, I was wondering," Teddy began cautiously.

"Always a good sign," Rose replied, bringing in the remnants of Howie's barely touched lunch. "Do you think your brother is feeling all right? He hardly ate a bite."

"Ah, he's fine," Teddy said, stuffing her wrist into a glass and twisting it around to scrape off some old milk. "If he didn't mope around a little and miss a meal, he'd be betraying Mom. Wrap it up," she added, indicating the sandwich, "he'll be starving in an hour."

"You, on the other hand, ate two sandwiches," Rose commented, scraping the crust corners off Teddy's plate.

"Me not eating won't get Mom safely back to Tacoma," Teddy replied, wiping the steam off the window over the sink. "Anyway, I was wondering . . . about the attic."

"What about it?" Rose asked, lighting a cigarette.

51

"Well, a house this size must have one," Teddy said cautiously.

"And?"

"And maybe you'd like to have me clean it. I mean, I'd even do it for free." *Too eager*, Teddy warned herself. *She'll get suspicious.*

"Clean the attic?" Rose asked skeptically. "What for?"

See? Now, tone it down, stupid! Teddy cursed herself before saying, "Well, attics are usually pretty dirty. How about that'll be a job for me and, if it's big enough and all, I could, you know, maybe fix it up some. Maybe make a reading room or something." *Good—reading room—how impressive . . . how academic.*

Rose grinned at her and said, "I thought I heard someone creaking around up there yesterday. How'd you even find the stairs?"

Oops.

"I, uh, opened the wrong door, I think, and . . ."

Rose's eyes seemed to be examining Teddy's face for sincerity, and Teddy, who could so easily lie to her mother, found Rose a more difficult target.

"Sure. Go ahead. Fix it up. Maybe while we're at it, I'll have a man come in to inspect the wiring. Don't want you rummaging around a firetrap."

"Damn it!" Teddy cried, seizing a cut finger and squeezing it. "I mean, darn it!"

"Ah no, our first injury," Rose said, going straight for her first-aid kit.

"It's not bad. Really," Teddy said, running cold water on the cut and cringing at the sting. "I see you keep your knives sharpened. Mom never does. She can't stand the sound of the grinding."

"Here, let me look."

"See? It's nothing. I'll watch out for the knives from now on, that's all," Teddy said, wrapping her finger and ignoring the throb.

Howie came in and asked, "What happened to you?" He demanded to see the wound, winced appropriately, reclaimed his sandwich and left.

"The sight of blood always makes him hungry," Teddy explained, winding a bandage around her finger. "See? Stopped bleeding already."

"Well, I hope this isn't setting the tone for the summer. Your mother told me you were going through your awkward period." Rose took Teddy's place at the sink. She carefully ran her hands through the dishwater, extracted the guilty knife and said, "Here's the culprit." She held it up and asked Teddy, "Want to get even?"

Intrigued, Teddy mumbled, "Huh?"

"There's a sharpening stone in that drawer."

Teddy pulled it out. Rose handed her the soapy knife and said, "Go ahead . . . dull that thing to within an inch of its life."

"You're kidding, aren't you? I don't need to get even with a stupid knife. I'm the stupid one for—"

"Oh, go ahead. Have some fun. Teach it a lesson."

So, hesitant at first, confused and curious about her grandmother's odd suggestion of revenge, Teddy sat and dulled the knife while Rose finished doing the dishes. It was a strangely satisfying experience . . .

the authorized destruction of a loyal implement gone wrong.

Later that afternoon Rose suggested that the kids walk into town and perhaps meet some of the locals, explore their new territory. Howie was up for it and teased Teddy when she hesitated. Under pressure from both sides and with the mission of running an errand for Rose, Teddy finally complied.

Howie had changed his shirt for the excursion. Before starting out, he looked at his sister.

"You wearing that cap?" he asked.

"You said I could have it," Teddy defended herself, tucking some loose hairs back behind her ears.

"You look stupid," Howie growled.

"What do you care?"

"Because I have to walk with you. Take it off." He took a swipe for it, but Teddy swiftly dodged him.

"Leave it alone!"

Howie looked at her rolled-up jeans with disgust, then grunted, "You oughta shave your legs, you know. Guys see hair, they think you're a dyke." And he started off without her.

She glared at him as he walked away, wanting to slug him with all the rage within her. She ran up to him, pulled him around by the arm, took off her cap, rustled her hair and shouted, "There! You think this looks any better?"

Howie looked at her hair, shook his head and said, "Put the cap back on. I couldn't care less, anyhow." He started walking away again.

She pulled the cap back on with an angry tug, rolled down her pants cuffs, then followed her brother.

They cut across Rose's backyard, crossed the bridge that crested the stream and, two blocks later, were in the middle of the humble center of Holiday Beach.

"Dare I risk crossing the traffic-choked street?" Teddy asked sarcastically. There was a car parked up the street and two trucks in front of the grocery store.

"Rose said most of the kids hang out at the penny arcade down by the turnaround," Howie said, pointing north. "I'm going down there."

"Count me out. I'm getting this stuff for Rose. Meet you back here?"

"Suit yourself." Howie started off, then came back and handed Teddy a key. "Here. The key to Rose's frozen-food locker. She said the door sticks and the peas are way in back." He crossed the street and disappeared around a corner.

Teddy waited for her brother the better half of an hour, clutching a bag of groceries, sitting on a sidewalk bench, feeling the frozen peas melt, knowing she looked like an idiot.

She went back into the grocery, asked for another sack, bolstered her courage and, with the groceries as her armor, walked toward the penny arcade.

She could hear the *ding-ding-dings* and repetitious honky-tonks of various amusements half a block away. The smell of popcorn and cheap treats greeted her as she approached the propped-open door. She adjusted her courage and her cap before venturing inside.

Kids were standing here, eating there, pounding machines, punching buttons and pulling levers. Somewhere from above, the Andrews Sisters were extolling the virtues of "Rum and Coca-Cola." Everyone was too busy to inspect Teddy's unimpressive arrival.

Naturally, Howie was at the machine farthest away from the entrance, and Teddy had to walk around several groups of kids to get to him. The second grocery sack was beginning to feel wet.

Howie was running up quite a score on his pinball machine. Three kids were watching him, kibitzing.

"I'm heading back" was all Teddy said.

Howie didn't look up, but he muttered, "Good."

"You coming?"

"Do I look like I am?"

Wang! Bong-bong-bong!

"He your brother?" a boy asked Howie.

"Yeah, but my brother's a sister. Feast your eyes," Howie muttered absently as he put a little elbow-english on the side paddles.

"Oh. Hi anyway," the boy continued, putting his cigarette to his lips to offer his hand. "Steve Maloney. I run this town."

"Baloney Maloney," another kid said, giving Steve a shove.

"You guys twins or something? You look alike," Steve commented, leaning into Howie's machine. Then he said to the others, "Hey—get a load of this—the Bobbsey Twins at the Seashore!"

Teddy avoided eye contact as she answered, "Yeah. You're *so* original. Look, Howie, I'm heading back." She turned to leave.

"So go," Howie retorted, still not taking his eyes off the electrical playground before him.

All Teddy wanted was to get safely out of the arcade before the soggy bags gave out. She would have made it except that as she turned to leave she bumped into a girl whose elbow jabbed her as she passed. The bag dropped. The groceries, complete with milk bottle, went crashing to the floor. The peas in their defrosted freedom rolled hither and yon, and all eyes, of course, were now on Teddy.

Kids laughed and jumped to avoid the escaping peas and the rising tide of milk. The plain brown paper that concealed a Kotex box was a dead giveaway. The proprietor was quickly upon her, handing her a broom and a dustpan, showing her the garbage can in the corner, trebling her agony. All he said was, "House rules, son."

It was, without a doubt, the most humiliating moment in the total of Teddy's fourteen years . . . social, domestic or fantasized.

EIGHT

The cool air off the ocean was a blessed relief on Teddy's face, still stinging with embarrassed anger. Walking wasn't fast enough—she had to run. So, once free of the high, troubling dry sand, she sprinted south toward Rose's. Baseball cap in her hand, hair tousled by the wind, she ran close to the water. She adored the sound of her sneakers as they hit the sand—step after sturdy step—she wanted to run forever—strides forever steady, breath forever easy, heart forever strong—forever and away from her summer, her family, her whole life.

She stopped when she came to the stream that ran next to Rose's house. She walked along its shore, and where it was deep enough, she waded into it, cleansing the salt water from her sneakers and splashing her face. It was startlingly cold—mountain-stream cold. She looked to the hills to the east, wondering how much colder still the water must be at its source.

The erratic course of the stream was a curious contrast to the steady, methodical, in-and-out reliability of the Pacific Ocean. It seemed to meander, north now, turn, now south, let's see, straight a little bit, now another turn north, as though teasing the awaiting arms of the ocean. Then, as it surrendered finally to the salt water, hardly anything of a stream at all . . . broken little brooklets of water, countless tiny islands and deltas, as though telling the ocean, "You may have me, but on my terms, as I am, and even then, only here and there."

Teddy forded the stream as far up as she could, until her calves ached with the coldness. Unable to bear it any longer, she climbed out and found that the shoreline itself was also hazardous to navigate. She had to climb among the large rocks, put there presumably to act as a retaining wall during storms. Logs were scattered everywhere, like matchstick toys tossed there by the giant, arrogant waves of winter storms. She walked to the bridge and inspected the construction of large, flat stones. *Holiday Beach takes its bridges seriously,* she thought as she looked through the dark, musty underside. As though to say, "Stop here and go no farther," there were three steel pilings placed vertically in the middle of the stream, protecting the bridge, the road and the town itself from storm-tossed logs.

She looked across the stream and saw Rose's house, nearly hidden among the gnarled pines. Teddy remembered the groceries she'd swept away at the arcade and started to formulate her story. She looked at the sun. It must be close to five o'clock. The grocery store would be closing soon, and then, of course, she couldn't be sent back into town. There. Safe. Simple. She'd stay down on the beach until it was after five. Walking back toward the beach, she whacked sand off her wet pants and tennis shoes.

She sat on a rock to dry, planning what she was going to write in her journal that night. First days are always hard, she knew that. She'd start off with something philosophical, something startlingly sage, then proceed to rationing out the blame and see what flowed from there.

A rock in the stream caught her attention. It was flat and just barely under the surface. *Probably slipperier'n snot,* she thought, *but what a great stepping-stone.* Then, looking up to the bridge behind her and back along the opposite side of the stream, she figured she could save herself nearly two blocks of walking if only there were a bridge, right here, across the stream. And that rock would be the first stepping-stone.

She looked around for more appropriately sized stones . . . just big enough for a foot and flat along the surface, of course. Hand-built bridges across anything had to offer some degree of danger, though. She had to build a bridge only the brave would attempt. Then, what fun to spy down from the widow's walk above and watch the attempted crossings . . . the spills, the close calls, the victories. She'd have to purposely place a stone that appeared sturdy but would tip or rock under a cautious foot. (A spill would serve such a person right, a just penalty for someone who would dare to trust someone else's bridge.)

It took her an hour to place enough rocks and driftwood across the stream. Wet anyway, she waded up and down the stream's shore, searching for the best offerings. She stood back, looking at her work, then took the first test, walking from rock to rock to rock with confidence and balance. Across and back. "Too easy," she said. Looking around, she found the perfect addition. A long, flat, heavy, weathered plank. She dragged it to its resting place—across the middle section of stepping-stones. It took some doing, but it finally came to rest and, as planned, offered the perfect temptation to someone wishing to cross the stream. Two more boards here and there for symmetry and a rotting one-by-four at the deepest part where the trespasser's courage must be greatest. Then it was finished.

When Teddy crossed her bridge and walked up to the house, it must have been long after six. Waiting for her there were Howie and Rose. No doubt he'd told Rose about the penny-arcade incident. No doubt she was in trouble. She'd offer to pay back the lost groceries through work, then simply tell them she was playing on the beach all this time.

She slipped off her sandy sneakers, swiped the sand off her wet pants and entered through the kitchen. "Hi," she said, testing the waters.

"Where've *you* been?" Howie demanded.

Unchallenged, Teddy looked coolly at Rose and replied, "Just right down there, on the beach." She had the sunburned neck and strained back to prove it. "Oh, sorry about the groceries. I'll pay it all back."

"Never mind about the groceries. I was worried about you. Howard thought you might—" Rose began.

"What?" Teddy interrupted, challenging her brother. "That I'd go out and slit my wrists? Just because every kid in the joint was laughing at me?"

"Actually, I was hoping you'd hang yourself," Howard mumbled.

"I couldn't give a damn what that bunch of creeps think!" Teddy snapped back at Howard.

"Well, you embarrassed the hell out of me," he bit back.

Rose positioned herself between them and spoke sternly. "You know, you two, when I was finally able to convince your mother to let you come down here this summer, I was hoping we could make up for lost time." She paused and looked at each twin. "Now, it's been just a little over twenty-four hours you've been here. I don't think any of us will live to August with this constant battle of yours."

"Sorry," Howie said, barely audible.

Rose turned to Teddy.

"Me too," Teddy mumbled in return.

"Now, I'm not asking you two to gush at the seams with undying love. All I ask is a little decency."

Silence. Then Rose continued. "I can't believe you two hate each other as much as you let on."

Neither Teddy nor Howard responded. They didn't even look at each other.

"Now Teddy," Rose said, "all you have to do is let me know where you are, when you'll be back and who you're with. Those are the only rules. Now, what kept you down there so long? Meet some kids?"

"I was just messing around in the stream," Teddy replied, running cool water over her sand-crusted cut finger.

"Town kids never play on the beach in the daytime," Howie offered expertly. "The tourists have it during the day. But the locals party down there at night."

"Tell me about it. Sometimes *all* night," Rose said, pulling a jar of corn out from the cupboard.

"So, do you think I can go?" Howie asked. Teddy could tell by the sound of his voice that he was looking innocent and hopeful, all in the same, smiling question. "Just a few kids, you know, a bonfire, hot dogs, singing, I guess."

"Where will you be?" Rose asked.

He pointed north and answered, "Just right across the stream."

"And who will you be with?"

"Steve somebody. I met him at the penny arcade."

"Baloney," Teddy replied.

"I did so! Oh yeah, Steve Maloney. Him and a kid named Benny and a girl, let's see, I think her name was Sally, then the grocer's daughter. I don't remember her name."

"Good kids," Rose admitted, now slicing tomatoes. "So, what's your curfew at home?"

Howie and Teddy simultaneously answered eleven and midnight, respectively. Rose looked at them, then decided on eleven-thirty.

"What about your sister? Is she invited?" Rose asked.

Howie looked at Teddy. She was a mess . . . partly sun-burned, dirty, smelly, sweaty, hair slicked back by her base-ball cap and her face even more freckled than just that morning.

Teddy read his mind and growled, "His sister doesn't care if she's invited or not. She couldn't care less about going to some idiotic beach yodel-fest." *Good*, she thought; *don't wait for rejection, do it yourself.* But it was true. She was aching, tired and simply wanted a deep, hot bath, fol-lowed by her friendly flannels, some hot tea perhaps, her journal on her lap, the latest news of the invasion of Nor-mandy.

"Do you mind being alone?" Rose asked. "Because if you

do, I'll stay home. I'll understand if you don't want to be in this mausoleum alone at night."

It hadn't occurred to Teddy that Rose would have anywhere to go, have anything to do, in a town the size of Holiday Beach, on a Saturday night. After all, she was a grandmother. Oh well, maybe bingo.

"Heck no, I don't mind being alone," Teddy replied. Actually, she cherished any moment to herself, especially when there was a mausoleum to explore.

"I'll just be a minute away. Down at Lou Lou's. A bunch of us old bats get together every Saturday night, drink a few beers, bring the war to an end. But really, Teddy, if you want me to stay here, your first night without your mom here and all, then . . ."

"I'm fourteen years old, Rose. Scared is the last thing I am."

Scared, of course, was the first thing she was as she waved goodbye to Rose, locking the door behind her. First, she pulled all the drapes to seal out the dark, they-can-see-you-but-you-can't-see-them world. There was no way, though, that she was going to soak in a tub, all alone in that huge, creaking, probably haunted house. She quickly dashed through a shower, then went straight to her flannels, robe and slippers.

Just as she was leaving her room, the sound of kids—teenagers—came lofting up through the windows. Laughing kids.

She turned off her lights and approached her window, carefully holding back the curtains. The beach fire was strong and snappy, the people encased in its light golden and warm. She strained to see her brother, but from a distance, they all looked the same.

As her eyes adjusted, she could see two girls dare a giggling attempt at her bridge. They were no match for the middle section, which quickly claimed the first girl. Laughter, shrill and feminine, came as the target stood, midstream, dripping fetchingly. The girl then ran, bare-legged, to the campfire, where she was welcomed with a blanket draping. Teddy smiled down, taking pity on the silly, wet creature.

She'd seen enough. Her bridge had worked its tempting magic. She let the curtains fall gently back into place and left her room. She went to the kitchen, boiled some water and finally, mug of tea in hand, began to explore. Or rather, snoop, if Howie were calling her game.

It seemed quite logical to begin where she'd left off: the library. She'd done the books, but awaiting her was the desk—always a proper choice. Without shame, she went through the drawers, getting a feel for the business side, if any, to Rosemary Dumont. Was she simply sitting pretty or deliciously loaded? Judging by the balance in a bankbook, she was set for life. Teddy found that information very comforting. Money was in the family, thank God. And a reconciliation between her mother and Rose was, well, started at least. Teddy made a mental note to work hard to encourage peace come August when her mother returned. Inheritances were at stake.

That resolved, she went back into the front room and browsed through Rose's record collection. The usual assortment—Miller, Lombardo, Shaw, the Dorseys. It told her nothing in particular.

From there, the baby grand in the corner. She ran her fingers lovingly up, then lovingly down. Her scarred hands seemed even more discolored resting on the black and white keys. She thought it odd that the piano was so in tune. Rose must play.

She opened the piano bench and flipped through the sheet music. Again, the usual assortment of rags and pops. She dug deeper. *Now what's this,* Teddy thought as she flipped through Chopin, Schubert, Liszt. *Why, Rose, you fool me again.* Then, at the bottom of the stack, Debussy. She carefully pulled out a worn copy of *"Clair de lune"* and placed it on the piano. She rubbed her fingers to warm them, then began.

The first chords were simple and familiar, but soon the melody became complicated. She didn't need the sheet music. She knew it by heart. Every adagio, every andante, every allegro. She barely kept up with the notes, feeling as though she were being pulled along helplessly by the building, the flowing, the ebbing of the familiar strain—as if she were so much foam upon a *clair de lune* wave.

How her father had adored this piece! Oh and how magnificently he had played it.

Unable to finish, she pulled her hands away and stared at the sheet music. She seized it, wanting to rip it to shreds. Then, gaining control of herself, she carefully put the sheets back inside the bench, in their place, at the bottom of the stack.

She wiped her nose with her robe sleeve and returned to her exploration.

There was a stunning armoire along the wall, and Teddy carefully opened it. It had been made into a bar, for there were mirrored shelves with fine glassware, decanters of liquor, napkins in one drawer, bar tools in another and in the large drawer toward the bottom . . . a scrapbook. It stared up at Teddy, the gilded words, "Family Memories." Dare she? Teddy reached down and pulled it out.

Sitting Indian-style on the floor, she lifted the cover. There were the usual pictures. Old, faded, some identified underneath, some missing, nothing spectacular. As the photos grew older, Rose grew younger. Teddy noticed a startling family resemblance: mother to daughter to daughter. Then some photos of a handsome man—a grandfather she'd never known.

It was a steely excitement for Teddy, going through the album, for there were no such things as dispatches from the past in their home. Everything had been lost. She was looking into the placid faces of her heritage for the first time.

She read each telegram, each letter, and all the other assorted memories that were tucked in haphazardly, no doubt with the promise of a proper pasting some future day. Then, toward the end of the book, another telegram, neatly folded and tucked securely into the binding. She pulled it out and it read:

```
Mrs. Rosemary Dumont
622 Roosevelt Avenue
Minneapolis, Minnesota


Mother—Begging you to come to Tacoma—don't
let me go through this without you—I'm in ag-
ony—please come help me—Delores
```

It was dated January 9, 1935. Thirteen days after the accident.

Then, not able to leave well enough alone, Teddy treaded further into the past. She found some newspaper clippings, folded, tucked away, yellowed by time and, please God, long ago forgotten. She unfolded the first, and its headline read "Society Matron Taken Ill—Daughter Rushes to Side of Eleanor Stokes—Constant Vigil." Teddy wasn't particularly interested. With shaking hands, she unfolded another article. Somehow, she doubted it would be some lost recipe or a "Katzenjammer Kids" cartoon; it was exactly what she had feared: the front page of the *Tacoma News Tribune*, dated December 27, 1934. Glaring back at her, in large, bold, faded letters:

CHRISTMAS FIRE CLAIMS FATHER, INFANT DAUGHTER

Her heart was pounding. She'd never read about it before—only heard about it, over and over and over. She was unable to read it in detail, word for word. Her eyes were only able to pick out key phrases . . . relevant phrases. That was all that mattered anyway.

> . . . Yuletide tragedy . . . heroic attempts to save infant . . . frantic mother . . . late-night tragedy . . . twin toddlers saved . . . entire home and its holiday contents lost . . . four-year-old daughter, Theadora Ann Ramsey, found by mother, only the day before, playing with matches . . .

Anger! At herself! Her vile discovery! Everyone! She threw the scrapbook across the room, scattering memories as haphazardly as the wind scatters fallen leaves. The scrapbook came to rest against a chair, pages flapping as though laughing at her. The front-page article landed at her feet. She grabbed it, wadded it up and threw it into the fireplace. She seized a box of matches and furiously struck several until one ignited. She threw it into the fireplace and watched as the newspaper burned until there was nothing left but lacy black ashes. Good—ashes don't tell.

Now, if only she could burn her memory.

NINE

Teddy awoke early the next morning, feeling in her muscles the memory of every rock, every plank, every exploration. At the foot of her bed was her journal, still open to the entry from the night before:

JE120—Sat nite late—I'm not going to say anything to anyone. Especially Rose. It's my own stupid fault for being such a damn snoop. Why would she keep that article, anyway? She's sick. Can't let go. Just like Mom. I'm just going to keep my mouth shut. I don't give a damn anyway!

The smell of Sunday breakfast was wafting through the house. Teddy beat Howie down to breakfast. Spam-and-cheese omelets, fried potatoes, spiced apples, homemade crullers.

"Morning," she said to Rose as she sat down in the breakfast nook. After the explorations of the previous night, Teddy found herself staring at Rose. She noticed once again how very different she appeared from two days ago when they first met. She was aching to ask why the absolute change, and as they chatted casually about this and that, Teddy searched for entrée.

Finally, it came, when Rose remarked, "I'm getting my hair cut Tuesday in Astoria. Want to make it a twosome?"

"Uh, I don't know. Mom says I shouldn't have it this short. She says with my neck I ought to have it longer," Teddy replied.

Rose flipped an omelet over with an expert twist of the wrist and asked, "And what does Teddy say?"

Suddenly, it was as though it were Rose seeking entrée, and Teddy took an extra slurp of juice as she thought about it. "Teddy says it doesn't matter either way," she replied, giving her grandmother a sideways glance. "Say, Rose, speaking of hair, just why did you wear that wig? I mean, pardon my saying, but wasn't that just a little bit, you know, phony?" *Take that, Granny!*

But Rose accepted the challenge, slopped the omelet onto her plate and said, sitting down, "Damn right it was phony. But you tell me: which Rose do you think your mother would find easier to talk to? The Rose I am today? Practically a stranger? Or the Rose she remembers from long ago?"

"Why should you care?"

"Because I'm her mother and I love her."

"Then why do you two always fight? Mom says you two never got along. That's love?"

Rose looked out the kitchen window and replied, "I was hoping we'd be different this time. . . ."

"Well, I just don't think you should wear the wig when she comes back," Teddy said when Rose paused, hoping if

she spoke with her mouth full, she would sound nonchalant.

"And why don't you?"

"I don't think Mom likes it when someone looks as good
as she does, you know what I mean?"

"You mean a daughter can model herself after her
mother, but a mother can't model herself after her daughter?"

That was a little more complicated than Teddy had antic-
ipated. After all, it was only a wig, some makeup and a pair
of perfect, prewar silk hose.

"Well," she said evasively, "I only know Mom's usually
the looker in the crowd. I thank my lucky stars I'm as
homely as I am. I'd hate to be beautiful, on top of everything else."

"On top of what 'everything else'?" Rose asked, smiling at
her granddaughter.

Now certain she was treading on precarious ground,
Teddy replied, "Well, you know. On top of everything else
she has to worry about. Job. Money. A man." There, she
thought, that just about covered "everything else."

"Oh." Rose nodded. "Doesn't your mother ever—"

Howie must have been listening from the dining room,
for his entrance was perfectly timed.

"Smells good in here," he said, giving his sister a sly
smile as he sat down across from her. "Omelets? Oh,
Spam."

"You eat it at home, you can eat it here," Teddy whispered at her brother.

Rose delivered his omelet and asked, "You all dressed up

for church, Howie?" Rose looked at Teddy, who was still in her bathrobe.

"Howie, you don't have to go to church here. I won't tell Mom," Teddy said.

"I want to go to church," Howie replied with a pious snap. "And what makes you think I won't tell Mom you're *not* going?"

"Howie," Rose broke in, "if you want to go to church, go to church. Teddy, if you don't want to, don't. Your mother didn't tell me anything about church. Simple as that. You do what you want in Holiday." Then Rose asked Teddy, "And what do you have planned for today?"

"I don't know. Maybe start on the attic."

"What attic?" Howie asked.

"My attic," Teddy returned. "Rose said I could clean it up, maybe make a reading room for me."

"Oh, that's real nice, Thea-door. Rose goes to all the trouble and money to fix us up rooms for the summer and what do you want? The attic. Mom'll love that."

"Well, why don't you just walk home and tell her?" Teddy shot back, leaning over and snapping off his clip-on and tossing it in his face.

"Knock it off!" Howie shouted, swiping across the nook at his sister.

"Is it always like this between you two?" Rose asked, for the first time raising her voice.

"Only when he's acting like Big Chief I'm the Boss," Teddy said, taking her plate to the sink.

"You know, Teddy," Rose said, "it's going to be a beautiful day. I hate to think of you in that hot, dusty attic on a day like this when the beach is filled with kids. Wouldn't you rather dive into your bathing suit and—"

"You wouldn't say that if you'd ever seen her in a bathing suit," Howie said, reapplying his tie.

Rose turned on him and said with a sharp smile, "You know, if I was a young man off to church presumably to seek God's forgiveness, I don't think I'd be building up such a list of things to be forgiven for. An hour may not be enough."

Wham! thought Teddy. *Take that, Howard the Coward!* She only wished her mother could have been there to witness it.

After breakfast, Rose put on her garden gloves and went outside to do battle with the weeds in her Victory garden. Howie left to seek an hour's worth of God's forgiveness, and Teddy took the bath she hadn't the courage to take the night before.

The light breezes that flowed into the bathroom from the open window cooled Teddy's sweating face and, to her relief, fogged up the mirrors.

Her eyes came to rest on a razor on the counter. She brought a leg up and noticed how dark her leg hair was getting. Back to the razor—her legs—Howard's acid words. Oh, what the hell? How much could it hurt? (In the process, she learned the stinging properties of soap and that blood didn't seem particularly thicker than water.)

Outside and below, she could hear children playing in the stream. She remembered her bridge, and, no doubt, all those who walked by were grateful for the passage her hard work was providing. Well, maybe she would go down to the beach for a while after all. See how her bridge was. Maybe collect a toll or two. Fortunately for all concerned, Teddy decided it was too cold for a bathing suit.

So, in baggy shorts, hairless, nicked legs, bare feet and a sleeveless old shirt, wet hair combed back, Teddy walked down to the beach. To her horror, a few stepping-stones here and there were all that remained of her bridge. The planks were gone, dragged away in the night in some hideous sabotage!

She waded the stream, walking through a set of children and their streamside sand play. In a sand dune up toward the grass stood her brother. He was looking out over the smoldering remains of a beach fire—the same one she'd spied down upon the night before. The closer she got, the more clearly she saw the partly burned remains of one of her planks and two others stacked next to it, awaiting their turn.

"Have fun in church?" she asked, startling him as she approached from behind.

"Never made it," he said absently, giving the plank a push deeper into the embers.

Teddy had suspected as much all along: holy as Howard had a tendency to be, even *he* wouldn't go to church without their mother's insistence.

"Hip-O-Crit," Teddy charged.

"Oh shut up. I would have gone to church if I'd found the right one."

"You think you're fooling Rose, but you're not fooling me."

"Get lost!"

"So what'd you do if you didn't go to church?"

"Hung around waiting for the arcade to open." He blew into the fire to bring it back to life.

"This was your fire last night, wasn't it?" she asked pointedly.

"Yeah, what's it to you?"

"And you guys used planks from that stream, didn't you?"

"Yeah. So what?"

"So those were *my* planks!"

"Well, I didn't see your name branded on them!"

"I built that bridge, Howie, those were *my* planks!"

"Ah, dry up," Howie said.

"You dry up!" she returned. She pulled him around and viciously grabbed at his tie as though to yank him to her face.

When the tie easily released in her hand, he laughed at her as she fell backward and landed flat, bringing her to a higher-pitched rage than before. She tackled him at the knees, and soon they were covered with sand, screaming and hitting, rolling dangerously close to the smoldering fire.

Howie landed on top of Teddy and sat astride her stomach, pinning her arms with his knees. He looked down at her and demanded, "Give?"

"Get off me, you asshole!"

He cleared his throat, gathered up a generous wad of spit and again asked, "Give?"

Out of the corner of her eye, Teddy saw that a few of the kids from the stream were now curious onlookers. Then one, the largest, simply walked past them, helped himself to one of the planks and began dragging it off for his own devices.

Teddy looked at Howie as he watched the small thief walk away with his prize. He released her, and together they sat, a sandy, panting mess, watching some eight-year-old brazenly steal the spoils of their war.

"Well, of all the nerve!" Teddy said.

"Yeah, what kind of upbringing's that little jerk had?"

"Beats me," Teddy returned, wiping sand off her legs. "Well, as soon as those little twerps go off to take their naps, I'm getting my planks back!"

"Yeah, me too."

Howie then noticed the hairless legs and the two telltale bandages on the knees. He pointed down and said, "I'll trade razors with you. The blade in mine is real dull."

To which Teddy said nothing.

They began walking back toward the house, giving the streamside children threatening scowls of impending revenge as they walked by.

"So, did you meet a girl or something last night?" Teddy asked nonchalantly, as she washed her feet off in the stream.

"Yeah, lots of girls. Steve's really cool. He knows everybody, even chicks down for just a few weeks. He thinks he might even get me a job fishing on his old man's boat."

"Hey, can he get me a job?" Teddy asked. "I can fish."

"Nah. This is out on the ocean. Deep-sea fishing. They don't let girls. You know how it is."

Teddy would have argued, would have challenged Howie's helplessness in bodies of water larger than bathtubs, but there was an understanding, a softness to Howie's voice that told her arguing was useless. "Yeah," she replied, looking out over the ocean, "I know how it is. Hell, you know me, I'd only puke anyway."

"Look, if you want, I could ask Brenda. Her dad runs the grocery. Maybe they need some help," Howie offered. "You'd like Brenda. She's all right. Kinda dumpy, but nice."

"Nah, that's okay. There's plenty to do at Rose's. That attic's gonna take some real work."

"Yeah, show me it," Howie said.

"It's my place, Howie. You can't horn in on it," Teddy warned, walking with him back up to the house.

"Oh, I don't want your stupid old attic. I just want to see it. Any good stuff up there?"

That reminded Teddy of the armoire, the scrapbook, the fire, the memory. Should she tell him? Tell him what her current investigating—snooping—had brought her? *No. Leave it alone, Teddy.* Howie had a history of falling apart whenever he tried to remember that night. That's why she'd made him promise not to talk to Rose about it. *Let it pass, Teddy. Just let it pass.*

TEN

Teddy and Howie were greeted at the house by a note pinned to the side door:

Kids:
If you need me, I'm at Blanche Seger's house, just a couple of blocks south, tying up newspapers for the cause. I forgot to mention it. Phone ES 221, one long, two short. Home around 4.

Love, Rose

"Guess what I found," Teddy tempted Howie as they helped themselves to leftover crullers.

"A personality," Howie mumbled through the crumbs.

"No, I'm serious. I found Rose's bankbook."

Howie stopped chewing and stared at his sister. "You were snooping again! What was the balance?"

"About fifty grand. And I'll bet she's got a stack of war bonds around here someplace too," Teddy said, her eyes growing wider at the prospect of knowing, let alone being related to, one so rich.

"No kidding?"

"Nope. How do you like that? We're poorer'n river rats all these years and ol' Rose is loaded. Just as I suspected. No wonder Mom wants to bury the hatchet," Teddy added, pouring herself a glass of milk.

Howie took the glass, downed most of the milk and said, "You can be so cruel, you know that, Teddy?"

"Well, you're the one always talking about being a lawyer. You think law degrees come in Cracker Jacks? That's why we're down here this summer, you dimwit. To get on Rose's good side. Pave the way for Mom."

Howie looked wounded to the quick, but he asked, "You think?"

"I don't think, I know. You want to see the attic or not?" Teddy asked, taking back her glass.

"Yeah, sure."

Teddy led the way up the steep staircase, the air growing warmer as they ascended. She carefully opened the door and said, "Remember, this is *my* place."

"Yeah, yeah," Howie grumbled as he walked past her and through the door.

Teddy tried to hold back her enthusiasm for the room. The more excited she appeared over the attic, the greater chance she had of losing part of its wealth to her brother. She showed Howie the large oval window that overlooked the ocean, with the treetops just below.

"Look at this." She cleared some boxes off the window seat and added, "Bet old ladies used to sit here for days and stare out to sea."

"To see what?" Howie asked, absently going through some stacks of old *National Geographic* magazines.

"To stare out at the ocean, you moron."

"So what are they looking for? Pirates? Japs? Their ship to come in? What? Ooo, tits!" he added, eyes widening as he gazed, amazed yet appreciative. "Sure love those African dress codes!"

Teddy looked out and just said, "What a creep."

"Huh?" Howie asked, coming back to the Oregon coast. "You're a creep."

"Why? Because I like to look at naked women? Let me see, here," he continued, flipping through the pages, "maybe we can find some naked men for you—"

"Oh, grow up!" Teddy snapped, grabbing his magazine and tossing it back down on the stack.

Howie pointed to the magazines and said firmly, "I want those magazines, Teddy. A few at a time, okay?"

"You pervert. You want to see the rest of this or not?"

"I want to see the rest of those!" he continued, going again for a likely-looking issue.

"All right, I'll sneak you down the damn magazines. Come here. Look at this."

"Oh yeah! The widow's walk!" Howie headed toward the steps up.

"No you don't. Me first." She opened the hatch and climbed up, followed by Howie. "I think it's just about the neatest thing," she said, looking down on the beach below.

Howie noticed how dotted white it was with bird tokens and said, "So do the birds. Does the telescope work?"

"I'm going to oil the hell out of it and see if I can get the

81

swivel working. But look, you can still see through it, only you have to look just down there."

Howie looked through it and said, "Those brats! Look, they've taken all our firewood we were stashing for the party tonight!"

"Let me see." Teddy looked through. "That wasn't your firewood, Howie. That's my bridge wood! You can't have it and neither can they!"

"Aw, who cares about your stupid ol' bridge?"

"All the people who use it!"

"Since when did you become such a do-gooder?"

"Wish those brats would stay on their own side of the stream," Teddy grumbled.

"That fuzzy-haired blond girl lives down here. It's more her stream than it is yours."

"How do you know?"

"That's Steve's little sister. I saw him walking her home from Sunday school. So quit thinking you own the whole bloody place, Teddy."

"I don't want the whole bloody place. I just want that stream."

Howie was starting to climb back down into the attic. "*And* this attic. Mom's right about you . . . always gimme, gimme, gimme. Now you're even thinking Rose's gonna give you all her money. . . ."

But Teddy couldn't hear him. She'd remained on the widow's walk, spying down on the children below. Howie stuck his head up and asked, "You listening to me?"

"No."

"Well, you can have this place. It's hot and boring up here anyway. Just don't come whining to me for any help."

"Shut up, shit ass!"

"Make me!"

"Come up here and I will!" Teddy said, still looking through the telescope.

She should have realized sooner that he would try to close the hatch and lock her out, and the hatch was nearly closed when she whipped around. She was able to get a few fingers on it, and she yanked at it, screaming obscenities at her brother.

He pulled, she pulled back. Then he let go, and Teddy crashed back with a scream. Howie heard the meek little fence crunch as Teddy fell into it. He scrambled back up to find his sister dangling half off the platform.

"Howie!" she cried out, clawing for a sturdier grasp.

He seized her by the arms and pulled up as hard as he could. The ancient shingles crackled as they broke away under her and fell silently to the ground.

Howie anchored his feet and pulled again, this time bringing his sister back onto the widow's walk. They both fell back, and Howie cascaded halfway down the steps and into the attic. Teddy, white and gasping for breath, was clinging to the hatch door.

Howie scrambled back around and grabbed Teddy by the wrist and held it tight, as though she were still in jeopardy of dropping.

"It's okay, Teddy. I have you." She was beginning to tremble, and he firmly tugged her forward. "Come on down, Teddy. We're all right."

"Shit, I broke the fence," she mumbled as she descended the steps with knees so weak she nearly fell again.

She sat weakly down on the last step, trying to regain her

breath. She and Howie simply stared at each other. Howie still tightly gripped her wrist. Several deep breaths, then, slowly, one growing on the courage of the other, smiles.

"Well," Howie said, finally letting go, "I ain't telling if you ain't telling."

"Tell what?" Teddy asked, leaning back on the steps, staring at the rafters, taking in more deep breaths.

"Honor Bright?"

"You can count on it."

"Say it."

"Honor Bright."

ELEVEN

JE121—*Sunday evening, late. I almost died today. No fooling—see? My hands are still a little shshshshakey. In almost dying, I learned a valuable lesson: Never fight with your brother on a widow's walk. Probably that goes for any other high place. It's a good thing Howie and me aren't afraid of heights, though, or else we couldn't have gotten that damn rickety fence fixed. I don't think Rose'll ever be the wiser. Well, at least Howie's had his fill of widow's walks and attics for a while. Good. Mine, all mine.*

Rose told us tomorrow should be nice. She just looks at the sunset and forecasts the weather. We'll see. She's not going to be too keen on me being up in the attic in the good weather. Guess I'll go back down to the stream tomorrow, anyway. I'll wear a hat. These damned freckles get bigger just knowing the sun's going to shine. Did I mention Howie saved my life? About time he did something for me.

Rose knew her sunsets. The morning was steamy with fresh-rising fog . . . as though the mist knew, the moment the sun hit it, that its reign was over, and it rose elegantly, then vanished obediently. The tide was low and away, barely visible, inaudible, and the shoreline rocks seemed high and dry, abandoned, seductive.

Howie and Teddy were excused from breakfast chores, and together they aimed for the beach . . . although Howie went south and Teddy went north. They met due west of Rose's house, and together they looked up, hands shading eyes, at the widow's walk.

"Looks okay to me," Howie said. "I can't tell. Can you tell?"

"Depends how often Rose looks up there," Teddy replied. "Who cares, anyway?" she continued, taking her gaze westward. "If she asks, dummy up, that's all."

Howie kept looking at the widow's walk. "Maybe a few new shingles on that corner, see, Teddy?"

Teddy sat on a log and broke up some sand clods with her toes. "Oh sure, you idiot, she's not going to notice some brand-new shingles. God, you're stupid."

"Screw you. I should have let you drop. That'd explain everything." Howie turned and started walking toward the rocks.

"Hey, where're you going?" Teddy called after him.

"Where does it look like?"

"You going to climb those?"

"You nuts? After last night? Nah, just going to explore. Rose said there's neat tide pools, sea enemies and stuff. You coming?"

"Sea enemies? What're those?"

Howie drew a blank and answered, "That's what I'm going to find out. You coming or what?"

Teddy considered the adventure. But already the rock was hosting low-tide explorers. She looked back up toward the house. The stream sparkled its own come-hither glances, and no one else was around to share them.

"Nah," Teddy called. "I'll be up at the stream."

"What're you gonna do? Collect more firewood for us?" Howie called back sarcastically.

"Aw, go make your sea enemies," she grumbled, wading into the stream and fording her way back up.

Her long colt legs took the stream with agile strides, and as the water got deeper, she simply plied more strongly against the cool, rushing waters.

When she was halfway up, she noticed how high the last tide line was. Along with its deposits of sea grass, twigs and pebbles, the ocean had taken the stream and divided it into two. She stepped onto the small triangle of newly formed delta. Three long, thin logs, mere toys in the waves' foamy grasp, had landed midstream, causing the split, the delta, the new land.

Any remains of her bridge, the rocks, the wood, the work, were ancient history now. Gone with one wave, replaced by three logs.

Teddy, in arrogant playfulness, turned to the ocean. "Oh, so you want to play rough, huh?"

So far away its murmur, so placid its surface, so delicate its waves. Yet Teddy heard it whisper back, "Yessss . . . yessss . . . yessss . . ."

She began to arrange the figures in her mind. Four tides a day, two high, two low. Twenty-four hours in a day, even on War Time. She looked at the ocean and calculated there were six more hours before high tide. She grinned, then challenged, "Bet I make it before you do."

She put more thought into calculating the tides than she did into her plan of attack. Before she'd even finished her challenge, she was pulling at one of the three logs that helped form the stream's split. She tugged, swore, tugged again. The log, once she'd lifted an end, was easier to ply around. Ignoring splinters and sea slime, she walked the log to its opposite side, where it unlodged, free of its compatriots.

Teddy tried to lift the log. Prying it was one thing, lifting it quite another. Dragging it then, using her long legs to fulcrum in her favor, she tugged the log into the "South Fork" of the stream. Using the strength of the water, she managed to maneuver the log until it crossed the stream. *One log, one bridge,* she thought to herself, satisfied, as she caught her breath. Now for the "North Fork," then a connector, and she was finished.

"Piece of cake," she mumbled. She paused to squeeze out a sliver, then began to attack the two remaining logs. The second was twice the size of the first, and Teddy looked around for other options.

Combing the sides of the stream, she once again began to build a stockpile of bridge parts. Logs, planks, rocks.

Several backbreaking hours later, while carrying a large plank toward the delta, Teddy noticed a shadowed form in the tall beach grasses. She damned the intrusion, but kept on walking. "Don't look at them, they won't look at you," she mumbled to the stream under her. "Keeeep walking, keeeep walking . . ."

She chanced a look over her shoulder. The intruder was still there, watching. "You have the whole beach. What the hell do you want to hang around a stream for?" she asked out loud, confident she couldn't be heard from that distance.

To her dread, the person started toward her. It wasn't Rose, she knew that, and Howie was up to his hips in sea enemies.

It was male, that she could tell. *Keep working,* she told herself. *He'll pass on by. Keep working.* She plopped the plank into the water and held her ground, as though being stream-splashed in the face was exactly what she wanted to have happen. Maybe the stranger didn't notice.

She ran her hands through her wet hair, replaced her hat and walked to the opposite shore to cast a nonchalant glance toward the intruder.

He'd sat down next to the stream, knees up, elbows resting, watching her tackle another plank.

Finally, he spoke. "Damming the stream?" he asked simply.

Teddy stood in the stream, legs astride the plank, wet, sandy, agitated. Who was this jerk, poking his nose into her affairs?

She didn't even look at him while she flipped back, "I'm cutting down on my swearing."

"I meant *dam,* as in Boulder, Bonneville, Grand Coulee."

Teddy pulled at the plank and grunted, "I knew what you meant."

"So, is that what you're doing? Building a dam?" he inquired further, this time walking to the stream's edge.

Teddy dropped the plank, stared across the stream. She

cocked her hat up to better see the boy, and he said, "Oh, it's *you*. The girl with the peas."

"Oh, it's you," Teddy echoed, stinging with the memory of the penny arcade. "Baloney Maloney."

"Yeah, but you can call me Steve."

"You should live so long," Teddy replied, half under her breath, wondering how rude she could be to him.

He watched her pull at the plank, shook a cigarette out of its pack, lit it, then playfully stepped on the opposite end of the plank.

"Do you mind?" she asked, looking up at him through her bangs, keeping her hands well below the surface of the water.

"Oh, I'm sorry," Steve said, offering her a cigarette. "How rude of me."

"Get off the friggin' plank!" Teddy growled.

Steve's eyes enlarged. He smiled, then stepped back onto the shore.

"Thank you," Teddy said, her face reddening as she strained to pull the plank free from the stream's current.

"Mind if I watch?" he asked, sitting back down.

"It's a free beach," she said, hating this boy, yet venturing a glance at him now and then. Even from a distance she could tell he was two, maybe three, years older. He was about her height, only thick . . . football, no doubt. Probably wrestling too; hell, maybe even cheerleading in a town the size of Holiday. She grinned at her supposition, stole another glance. He was as sandy as the beach around him . . . tan, gritty, golden. *Fast*, she thought. *Bet he's . . . fast.*

"Actually, I prefer to think of it as *my* beach," Steve said, taking a drag on his cigarette. "But that's okay. Go ahead. Build your damn dam."

"I'm building a bridge, not that it's any of your beeswax," Teddy said, abandoning the plank and lifting a rock instead. She dropped it in place and, once again, was baptized with water.

Steve laughed and said, "Any moron can build a bridge." Teddy made no reply, but kept on with her task, wishing he would get lost.

"Why, if I had a dime for every bridge kids build down here in a summer, I'd be rich," Steve continued.

Knee-deep in water and trying to extract a large rock, Teddy ignored his comment. She tried not to grunt, but she knew the moisture on her face was now more sweat than water.

"Yessir, anybody can build a bridge. Now a dam. That takes real talent."

"Look, if you want to sit and smoke and be a pain in the neck, why don't you go back to your penny arcade? I'm sure someone there thinks you're a regular Bob Hope."

"You summer kids are all alike, you know that?" Steve continued, seemingly unoffended.

Teddy kept pulling, tugging, swearing.

"Nobody thinks about the high tides. Sand castles, bridges, love letters . . . swoosh! All gone with the next high tide. You're all idiots."

Teddy stopped and looked at Steve. Then, as she rested, she looked around at the previous high-tide line. He was right. She was an idiot. She looked back out at the ocean, which, right on schedule, wasn't nearly as far, nearly as lifeless, as it was when she had started.

Steve finished his cigarette and flicked it just upstream of where Teddy was standing. She watched it float toward her, then catch on the dam the high tide had created.

"A dam, huh?" she asked him.

He leaned casually back onto the sand and looked at the ocean. "A dam," he replied with a cool confidence. "And if you wanted real action, you'd build it way up there, close to the bridge. Summer tides never make it up that far, unless there's a storm, of course."

"Then what?"

"Then it's every dam for himself."

Teddy followed his gaze and shaded her eyes. "That close to the bridge? But, wouldn't a dam up there—"

"Flood the bridge?" Steve finished for her. "It's only been done once. My brother Harry flooded the bridge in thirty-eight." Then he looked her over carefully and added, "But I wouldn't worry about that. I doubt a girl could build that good a dam. On second thought, maybe you ought to stick to bridges."

She crossed the stream, where each of them got a better look at the other—he leaning back on thick arms, she with hands in pockets. She looked down at him; he appeared even more golden in her shadow.

"I could build a better dam than you could," she said. He smiled up at her, and she cursed her buck teeth and the bands that tried to control them, for she wanted like hell to smile back.

"That a challenge?" he asked.

"Yeah, that's a challenge."

"All right," Steve said, taking his shoes off, then wading the stream. He walked several paces up, stopped in the middle, turned and said to Teddy, "Halfway. We both build. Best dam by . . . how long you down for?"

"Middle of August."

"Best dam by say, August first, wins."

Teddy walked across to her side of the stream as though to defend her territory. "You got a deal. Wins what?"

"Bragging rights. Best Damn Dam of 1944. Deal?"

He waded toward her and stretched out his hand.

She eagerly took it, gave it the strongest shake she could and replied, "Bragging rights. Deal."

He looked down and saw her scars, and she slowly extracted her hand from his, wondering if this kid merited an explanation.

But he didn't say anything.

Nor did she.

TWELVE

Constructing a dam called for supplies: shovel, rake, wheelbarrow and, of course, gloves. Teddy went straight to the basement, where she recalled seeing all these implements. Hearing the first ring of the telephone upstairs reminded her that perhaps she should ask Rose before taking the necessary tools. Hearing the second ring reminded Teddy she hadn't thought about her mother once that day. Skipped her clean—from Rose to Howie to Steve to dam.

Guiltless, she lightly took the stairs up until, toward the top, she paused to eavesdrop on the telephone conversation seeping through the open kitchen door.

"Oh hello, Delores . . . well, we're just fine. . . . How was your trip? . . . Uh-huh . . . uh-huh. . . . What happened then? . . . Oh no, what did you do? . . . Well, lucky for you that truck driver came along then. . . . Good . . . I told you, they're fine. . . . No, they're both down on the beach. . . . No, they're not exactly pining away. . . . Oh, I guess Howie was a little blue just after you left, but he came around. . . ."

Rose must have walked toward the dining room, for Teddy had to lean closer into the door to hear.

". . . Yes, now that you mention it, I guess I do detect some problems . . . but nothing that . . . nothing that . . . nothing . . . dammit, Delores! Will you let me finish? . . . I really don't think you have anything to worry about, dear. Teddy is a lovely girl. . . . Oh, how can you be so cruel? I remember you going through an ugly period. . . . Well, the more you make her wear those damn gloves, the more she's going to think she has something to hide!"

On long-distance cue, Teddy pulled her hands into her sweatshirt sleeves. She didn't have to imagine what her mother had said: nothing she hadn't been told to her face. She grinned upon hearing her grandmother slash back at her mother, but her smile quickly faded when she heard Rose's next words.

"No, I don't think she needs professional help, Dee Dee. In fact, I think she's the last one in the family who needs . . . Oh, do you really? Well, I'll tell you what, dear, I have them for the summer and we'll just see. . . . I mean it, Delores, stay where you are. Don't come running back down here. Everything is just fine."

Teddy leaned into the stairwell while Rose took an apparent barrage from the other end of the line. It must have been quite a speech, for Rose remained silent for what seemed to Teddy like a week. "Come on, Rose," Teddy whispered to the door, "let her have it! She's your daughter . . . tell her off!"

She dared to push the door open a little farther to see Rose, imagining her to be pacing, fuming, gathering ammo while her daughter ranted. She peeked around the corner

and saw her, leaning into the threshold, smoking a cigarette and appearing as casual as though she were listening
to nothing more extreme than the operator's monotoned
"at the sound of the chime. . . ." Finally, Rose was allowed
to speak.

". . . Yes, Dee Dee. I know, I know. I realize I've only
known them a few days. . . . You're right. . . ." Then,
practically singing, "You're absolutely right." *Odd,* thought
Teddy, *the sound of victory, the words of surrender.*

Then Rose's voice suddenly softened, and Teddy had to
strain to hear.

"Oh, Dee Dee, please, when are you going to stop living
in the past? Don't you know 'Nothin' changes nothin''?
. . . That may be, but how can the wound heal if you keep
picking the scab? . . . Well, I'm sorry, but that's what it's
like . . . a lot of picking, no healing."

Another pause, a long one. Then, ". . . Oh, you're welcome, dear. . . . Well, where would I wear them in Holiday
Beach? . . . No, just take the money and buy yourself
something nice. . . . No, I'll take the kids up to Astoria and
buy them school clothes in a few weeks. That money is for
you. Please, just leave the kids to me, Delores. This is your
fun time too, you know. . . . Well, dear, this is your nickel.
. . . Yes, yes I will. . . . No, don't worry about that. I'll
have the kids call you next Sunday, how's that? . . . Now,
from now on, if you have to call, call collect. . . . No, I
insist. . . . Yes, I'll tell them. . . . Goodbye, dear."

Teddy ducked back into the stairwell and started to creep
back down the stairs. She heard Rose's footsteps approach.
The door opened wide, and Teddy froze, midstep, mid-
flight.

"Your mother says, 'Be good, don't swear, be a lady, keep your gloves handy, and for God's sake start using a little makeup,'" Rose announced flatly.

Teddy looked up at Rose and asked sheepishly, "That go for Howie too?"

"She also said, 'Don't be a smart mouth,'" Rose continued, smiling down at Teddy's impertinence.

Teddy backed down a step and replied, "Some things you can change, some things you can't."

Rose sat on the top step, making them now eye-to-eye. She exhaled six perfect smoke rings and said, "You know, as much as you hate to admit it, she does love you."

Well, enough of this, thought Teddy. *No eye-to-eye, no heart-to-heart, not while there are streams to be damned.* "Probably," she answered swiftly, starting back down the steps. "Say, Rose, suppose I could borrow a pickax and some boots? Got a steam shovel anywhere around here?"

"What for? Finally going to bump Howie off?"

"I'm going to build a dam, but a pit for Howie would be fun too," Teddy replied, placing a pair of rubber boots along her foot for sizing. "What size are these?"

"Seven." Rose opened her pants cuff and flicked cigarette ash into it.

Teddy took down a clam shovel from the rafters and held it up. "Can I use this?"

"What about the attic?"

"Thought I'd use a broom for the attic," Teddy said absently, carefully taking down a pickax.

"I mean, smart mouth, I thought you were going to clean out the attic for me."

Teddy plastered her hair back under her cap and looked

up at Rose. "Thought you didn't want me wasting all this nice weather in the attic," she countered.

"Wheelbarrow's in the greenhouse" was Rose's reply as she stood up. "A dam, eh? That poor stream. What it takes during the summer. Most kids build bridges."

"Bridges are for sissies."

"Go ahead. Take what you need, but leave any of it on the beach and I'll . . ."

Teddy rested the ax on the floor and gave Rose her full attention for the rest of the threat. "Yes?"

"I'll tell your mother," Rose added, smiling wickedly. She squished out her cigarette on the top step, picked up the butt and closed the basement door behind her.

From there, Teddy found the wheelbarrow, loaded it with her supplies and trudged down the sandy path toward the stream.

She had imagined Steve the Dam Rival to be hard at work on his side of the stream. But he was nowhere to be seen as she crested the ridge and looked up and down the stream. The beach was beginning to entertain late-morning arrivals, and several small fishing boats dotted the ocean. Then she remembered that Steve fished with his father. *All the better*, she thought as she dumped out the contents of the wheelbarrow. *Head start. Great.*

Rocks. First rocks. She went to the remnants of her bridge and began pulling out those most memorable to her—old friends, familiar faces. She pulled, tugged and begged them forth as though they were obligated to walk from the stream's bed to their new home as the dam's foundation.

The tide was still rising, and the gentle summer surf

seemed to prefer riding the stream up, clearly cheating, finding the flow easier water upon water than it was on the warm, dry, troublesome sand. Cold as the stream water was, the ocean water was colder still on Teddy's legs. She bent over, pulling at a stubborn rock when the tide met her. Then, as though lending a hand, the salt water ate away the muddy suction and, with only one last, vague tug, the stone complied, and it was once again Teddy's—to steal, to place, to build.

She rolled it onto the shore, then, using all her strength, hoisted it into the wheelbarrow with its mates and, neglecting to thank the power of the tide, wheeled the bounty away.

"So what do you think you're doing?" Howie asked bluntly, startling Teddy.

She looked up, found her brother's shadow against the late-afternoon sun and replied, "Nothing you'd care about."

"Building another stupid bridge?"

"I'm building a dam." Teddy pulled on a pair of gloves and began rolling a large rock toward the stream.

"A damn what?"

"Very funny. Why don't you go up and fix us some sandwiches?"

"I already ate."

That brought Teddy around. "When?"

"I ran into Steve down on the beach. I ate at his house."

"You did? But doesn't that Steve guy fish with his dad?"

"Yeah. What's it to you?"

"Well, did he say anything about him building a dam? Him and me got a bet going."

99

Howie turned and laughed. "Now what person with half a brain would want to waste their time doing something stupid like that? Outside of you, that is. Come to think of it, since you don't even have half a brain, don't let me stop you."

He turned, but Teddy, with impeccable timing, called him back. "Howie. Mom called."

"She did? When?"

"Couple of hours ago."

"Why didn't you come and get me?"

"It was her nickel, and you were somewhere making sea enemies."

"So? You could have called me. You could have rung the bell. What'd she say? She get home all right?"

"I didn't talk to her," Teddy said, returning to her stream.

"Why not?" he pursued.

"Because I was eavesdropping and didn't want Rose to know."

Howie seemed to accept this as normal behavior for his sister and asked, "Well?"

"Well, I heard Rose say she's going to buy us school clothes."

"New?"

"Yeah."

"Brand-new? Not just new-to-us-new?"

Teddy started hauling another rock.

"What else did you hear?"

Teddy hesitated, then replied, "They got into an argument. Over us."

"Bad?"

Teddy shrugged and continued rolling the rock.

Howie approached her and said, "Come on, you little jerk, what else?"

"How should I know? I only heard Rose's side."

"Was she upset?"

"Rose?"

"No, Mom. Was she crying?"

"Probably."

"Aw, shit."

"Look, Howard, you're going to get an ulcer worrying about Mom. Here," she added, hoisting a rock and handing it to her brother, "get your mind off it."

Howie held the rock, unsure whether to drop it or follow his sister's instructions. "Where does this go?" he finally asked.

"Over here," Teddy said, dropping her own large rock into the stream.

Howie complied and dropped his rock alongside Teddy's.

"Think we ought to call her?" he asked.

"Mom? No."

"I'm going to . . ." Howie looked up toward the house.

"Look . . . Howie, Rose said we'll talk to her on Sunday. That's soon enough. Mom needs this time to herself."

"Since when do you care what Mom needs? Just two days ago you'd sooner cut off your right nut than think of what Mom needs."

"I don't have a right nut."

"Right knocker, then."

"Don't have one of those, either."

"Don't change the subject!"

Teddy faced him, picked up the shovel and said firmly, "Look, things have changed, that's all."

"Yeah?" he challenged. "Since when?"

"Since Rose. So leave Mom alone. Sunday's soon enough for her."

That was that. Teddy turned her back and plunged the shovel sharply into the wet sand.

THIRTEEN

"Any sand left on the beach?" Rose asked through the kitchen window, watching Teddy wash her legs off with the garden hose.

Teddy was startled, then located Rose in the window. "Some."

"Finish your dam?" Rose lit a cigarette and stood in the doorway.

"Barely started. Howie around?"

"But you were working on it all day."

Teddy turned off the hose, coiled it and looked up at her grandmother. "Doesn't have to be done until August first, Rose."

"Why August first?" Rose asked, absently tugging at some beach grass that had found its way into a small bed of snapdragons.

Not sure how much to disclose, Teddy replied, "Um . . . well, I'm sort of . . ."

As usual, Howie's timing was impeccable. He rounded

103

the corner of the house and took no time or shame in finishing Teddy's answer for her.

"She's got a bet or something going with Steve Maloney."

"Who asked you?" Teddy barked.

Howie took his turn at the hose, and when Teddy suggested he keep his nose out of her business, her damn dam, he turned the hose on his sister. Rose got out of the line of fire and watched from the safety of the kitchen.

The twins finally presented themselves at the kitchen door, wet, dripping, exhausted. Rose handed them towels and said, "Gee, I hate to waste clean kids. How about we go out to dinner? Go change. I'll warm up the car."

"Do I have to wear a dress?" Teddy asked, as though to suggest that if she did, she wasn't going.

"I've already told you, this is the beach. Do as you please," Rose replied, smiling. "I do."

Rose took them to Sadie's Kitchen just south of town. The place, small to begin with, was packed, so they had to wait for a booth. Teddy and Howie both looked for a familiar face, but it was Rose who seemed to know everyone. The more people Teddy was introduced to, the more she pulled in, the less she smiled, the deeper her hands plunged into her pockets. Everyone made comments on how much she and Howie looked alike. How lucky Rose was to have them the whole summer.

When the food came at last, it was wonderful. The chicken was steaming, crispy, juices easing out. Mashed potatoes awash in country gravy. Even the peas tasted wonderful.

"Look at her go," Howie grumbled, watching his sister attack her dinner.

Teddy shot him a dirty look, and Rose quickly cut her off. "How's your chicken, Howie?"

"Fine. Jeez, Teddy, ever hear of a knife?"

"Howard," Rose warned. "Now, maybe you better tell me more about this fishing job."

"Well, Steve says it's just off and on. Just when his dad can get the gas and get across the bar. You know. Lots depends on things."

Teddy just ate and listened to the conversation.

"Maybe we better see how your mother feels about your fishing out on the ocean," Rose suggested.

Howie jumped in with, "Oh, she won't care."

"Like blazes she won't," Teddy said. "She'll say it's too dangerous. She thinks everything you do is too dangerous."

"Well, commercial fishing is. That's why we better ask her," Rose continued.

"Really, Rose, she won't care. If we tell her, she'll just worry. All Mom ever does is worry. This is her vacation too, you know."

"Vacation from worry? A mother? Ha!" Rose commented dryly, sipping from a glass of beer.

There was something in her voice, a wryness, a sadness, which made Teddy look at Rose and made Howie back off for a moment.

Then, softer, logically, Howie said, "Well, it's a big boat, Rose. I'll wear a life jacket and everything. It's good money, and in a way, I'm doing it for the war effort."

"How so?" Rose asked.

"Well, the more fish we eat, the more beef for the soldiers."

Rose turned to Teddy and asked, "What do you think?"

"I think if the Japs win, we'll *all* be eating fish," Teddy mumbled as she swiped her plate with a piece of bread.

"No, about Howie fishing," Rose said.

"Him fishing?" She looked across to her brother, and all she could see was herself—with the house to herself, with the stream to herself and with Rose to herself. "Work'll do him good."

"And what about your mother? Should we ask her?"

Teddy looked at Howie again. His jaw was hard, his lips tight, his eyes in a set, I'm-warning-you stare. How well Teddy knew that look . . . how identical it was to hers on a million occasions.

"Nah. Howie's right, Rose. Mom'll worry herself into a coma. It's her vacation. He'll be careful. Besides, bet all they'll have him doing is cutting bait or cleaning puke," she added wickedly.

"When do you start?" Rose asked.

"He said Thursday they'd go out," Howie replied, rounding third base.

"All right. You can start. But we *will* tell your mother when we call Sunday, got it?"

He agreed, then dove into his pie à la mode with a certain victory.

Walking back to the car after dinner, Teddy grabbed Howie by the jacket and pulled him back.

"Hey, knock it off!"

Being a fast learner, Rose kept on walking.

"Didn't you forget to mention just one little thing?" Teddy asked.

"No."

"How about the fact that you swim like a brick?"

"I don't either."

"You're right. Bricks swim better. Wonder what Rose would say if she knew you couldn't swim your way out of a fishbowl?"

Howie was taking the potential betrayal seriously, and he lowered his voice accordingly. "Come on, you're not going to say anything, are you?"

"Did you tell Steve and his dad you can't swim?"

Rose honked the horn.

"Hell no. I can't tell Steve I can't swim, Teddy. Come on, you know how it is."

"Well, what about when Rose tells Mom?"

Howie had indeed put some thought into it. "I'm going to tell Mom I spent all my spare time learning to swim."

"Yeah, sure."

Another honk of the horn.

"And I will too. Only, I got to learn when none of the other kids are around, you know? Maybe you and me, we can . . ."

"Oh no, keep me out of this. I tried teaching you last summer, and you almost drowned me."

"You owe me, Teddy. Remember the widow's walk?"

"Oh, great, so I'm going to pay for *that* my whole life?"

A third, long honk.

"Aw, come on, Teddy, have a heart."

"What's in it for me? I teach you and you earn all the money, huh?"

"All right, I'll pay you to teach me."

"Want better. Want ten percent."

"Ten percent!"

The fourth honk was the deadliest-sounding of all.

"Make that twenty percent," Teddy said with a cool smile. "Take it or leave it."

"I'll take it," Howie said, resigned. "But we go to the lake, after dark, when I say. Got it?"

He climbed into the backseat, judiciously leaving the front seat for Teddy. She climbed in, and Rose said, "For your future reference, this car will leave on the second honk."

"Sorry," Howie said, looking at Teddy.

"Well, whatever it was, I hope you settled it."

Teddy looked back at Howie and replied, "Yeah. We settled it."

Howie nodded slightly and looked out the window.

Angry clouds on the horizon and sparring southern winds foretold rain, and Teddy looked forward to the stormy darkness ahead. The phone was ringing when they entered through the kitchen, and Teddy was first to reach it.

"Oh, hi, Steve," she said.

Howie, upon hearing this, grabbed the phone from her, saying, "It's for me. Hi, Steve. . . . Just walked in . . . huh?" He turned toward his sister and said, "Steve says to tell you your dam's a goner."

"Tell him he can . . . ," Teddy began. Rose made it a point to walk between her grandchildren on the way to the dining room.

"He says a storm's coming," Howie continued. He waited

until Rose was out of earshot, then repeated in a low voice, deliciously, "He says you are skeee-rooooed."

"Tell him my brother can't swim," Teddy growled.

Whereupon Howie quickly changed the subject. "So what's up? . . . Tonight? . . . But what about this storm? What's a storm fort?"

Teddy pricked up her ears.

"Neat! Yeah . . . Oh, I don't know about that. I don't even know where she keeps the stuff," he whispered, taking the phone along as he searched a few cupboards.

Teddy went to the appropriate cupboard, opened it up, then showed her brother the contents: wine.

He smiled at the discovery and told Steve, "Never mind. All set. Now, where's this place? . . . Great . . . Huh? What for? . . . Yeah, okay, see you there."

He looked at Teddy, then hung up the phone.

"He says you can come along, if you want."

"Where?"

"Storm fort. That's where the local kids party when it rains."

"Why?"

"What do you mean, why?" Howie asked, taking a bottle of wine and putting it into his pants, pulling down his sweatshirt to conceal it. "Because . . . I don't know, because it's a party, that's why."

Teddy followed him upstairs with the question, "No, I mean why does he want me to come?"

This also stumped Howie. He looked down at his sister on the landing and simply shrugged. "For a laugh?"

She changed her mind about the storm fort ninety-three times in a split second. On the ninety-fourth time, she'd decided that the intrigue of a storm fort was stronger than was the possible degradation of associating with her peers.

Rose granted clearance. And, although Howie grumbled about it, he waited for his sister outside on the front steps, bundled and slickered against the impending storm, wine bottle securely fastened to his side.

FOURTEEN

Clean jeans rolled up to the calf, saddle shoes, red-and-blue plaid under sweater vest, slicker, tam hat taken off the coatrack. Teddy knew if she'd taken too long to get ready, Howie would have teased her about it. As it was, she looked presentable. Besides, it was dark, windy, rainy. Who cared, anyway?

"About time," Howie grunted as Teddy appeared.

Teddy said nothing but walked down toward the stream.

"Hey, dumbo, where're you going?"

"To the beach."

"Well, it's this way," he said, indicating south with an impatient flick of his head. He started off without her, and she followed, wondering what she was getting herself into. Storm fort. Probably a sandpit. Big deal.

They dredged the high beach sand, fighting the southerlies. A lone light blinked out from the swaying trees in their path ahead. Howie stopped.

"Steve said it was just south of that streetlight. He said they fly a flag of some kind when the kids are in the fort."

Teddy kept walking, but Howie pulled her back.

"Wait a minute, ugly. I just want to make one thing perfectly clear right now. These are *my* friends, got it?"

"So?"

"So don't screw up—say or do anything stupid like you usually do. And Steve's taken. Not that there's a chance of a snowball in hell he'd be interested in you."

Teddy knew just how to respond. She chucked his prickly chin and said, "Sure. I get it. You saw him first. When you two want to be alone, just give the high sign and I'll make like a tree."

She grinned at him and turned toward the streetlight. Howie, on the other hand, had never learned just how to respond.

"You take that back!" he hollered.

"Make me," she replied confidently.

He whirled her around again, and Teddy simply said, "Twenty-five percent."

Howie glared at her, then let go, and they walked the remaining distance in almost total silence, Teddy quietly smug, Howie quietly swearing.

The flag was indeed flying, although the high-and-mighty flag was a pair of soggy, holey long johns and the pole was a thin, wind-weakened fishing rod. A small, smoldering fire was struggling to survive against the wind and rain.

"Some fort," Teddy mumbled.

"Hey! Steve!" Howie called out into the hillside, straining his eyes into the shadows of the trees and sand dunes.

There was no reply save the wind.

"You've been had, Howie."

"Hey, Steve?" Howie called out again.

This time, Howie's call was answered by a beer bottle swooshing past them, landing neatly in the center of the fire.

"Where are you?" Howie called into the hillside.

Then a large shadow moved in front of them, and silhouetted suddenly with light from behind, Steve stood, holding back an old rug that guarded the entrance among the thick beach pines.

Steve didn't move but solemnly asked, "What's the pass word?"

"Ub-b-b, ub-b-b-b," Howie stammered, caught off guard. Then he pulled out the bottle of wine, held it high and said, "Manischewitz!"

"Enter," Steve allowed, taking the wine, stepping aside and allowing Howie to enter. But as Teddy tried to follow, he stood in front of her and repeated the query.

"What's the password?"

Teddy looked up into his darkened face. The only thing she could think of replying was, "Grand Coulee."

Steve considered this, then replied, "Yeah. Why not?" He allowed her to pass but added, "But next time, you have to bring something to drink, okay?"

"Yeah, sure."

The storm fort was more of a cave, cut deep into the hillside. It was damp, cold, held together by roots, driftwood, old planks and positive thinking. Blankets were laid out, and there were several makeshift stools to sit on.

Steve held the wine bottle up and asked, "Who's got the pain?"

Every kid in the storm fort responded on cue, "I do! I do!" Steve tossed the bottle to the nearest kid, and it was passed around.

"All right, guys," Steve began, "this here is Howie Ramsey from the other night. His twin sister, Heddy was it?"

"Teddy," she corrected. She shyly acknowledged the kids in the storm fort and wondered what the hell she was doing there.

"Right. Food's there, booze there, cigs where you can bum 'em," Steve continued, displaying the fort's bounty of swiped party staples.

"What? No orchestra?" Teddy asked flatly.

And for the first time since puberty, Teddy elicited laughter from her peers—not the stinging, humiliating kind, the kind she had come to know so intimately, but the "hey, that's funny" kind.

She smiled and was bid welcome to the storm fort.

It was strange, watching her brother drink. She knew he did it as often as he could, but still, she'd never witnessed the actual downing of beer or wine or a combination thereof. Strange also was watching Howie melt into a different person and into the affections of some local girl.

As the couples formed, as the fire outside was built up, as the confines grew damper, as the beer and wine did the talking, as the evening wore on, Teddy was more and more uncomfortable. No doubt because she was the only one not drinking, she convinced herself.

Out of the corner of her eye, she watched Steve. Ruddy now with the glow of the lanterns, the glow of the booze, the glow of, in his words, owning the town. He clearly owned the storm fort, its contents, its inhabitants. Steve was holding court, and those around him adored him. They laughed at his tipsy antics, and all talk was centered around, by, or through him. A few girls, not yet paired up with a boy or a blanket, flirted mercilessly with him, and he seemed to be more than capable of handling such adoration.

So, when Steve turned to Teddy and asked softly, "Say, you having fun?" no one was more shocked than she.

"Yeah, sure. I'm a little tired, though. Think I'll head on back." She couldn't remember a time when she was speaking so close to a boy, save Howie in their nose-to-nose combat. He smiled at her, and although she fought it, although she damned it and forbid it to occur ever again, she felt her heart beat faster.

"Ah, come on, it's early. Stay," he coaxed.

"What for?" *Stupid! Stupid! Stupid!* she screamed at herself.

But Steve smiled at her simple question, as though having heard it for the first time. "Uh," he began, running his hand through his hair, "well, I know. Because, because we haven't talked about Grand Coulee, that's why." He indicated the wind picking up outside and added, "I'm afraid you're . . ."

"Skeee-roooed?" Teddy asked.

Steve grinned and said, "Well, yeah."

Teddy listened to the wind sing through the musty old rug. "Really? I don't think so. I'm doing a double foundation. I'm not worried." She tried to look confident but was more concerned about looking plain stupid. What the hell was a double foundation?

"Tell you what," Steve said, pulling Teddy up to her feet. "Let's me and you go look."

Well, she was planning on leaving anyway, and she'd just as soon not walk home alone.

Steve kicked Howie's feet, interrupting him from his impassioned conversation with his sweet local. "Taking off for a while, buddy."

Howie looked up and saw Teddy standing by the entrance. "With her?" he asked.

"Going to walk her home," Steve said, grinning. "She'll be okay. Promise."

But the look Howie threw his sister implied he was anything but concerned about her safety. She'd leveled many a bully in her day.

Teddy returned his look and knew, just knew, he was impressed.

"Hey," he said, lifting his beer bottle to her. "Take it easy, Sis."

FIFTEEN

The cool rain and the breeze that delivered it were a welcome relief to Teddy's flushed face. How she adored escaping.

"Watch your step," Steve said, lighting her way down the sandy slope with a flashlight. It seemed most natural he'd offer his hand for support, but Teddy, out of habit, jumped down off the last log and landed unsteadily next to Steve. She wavered in the wet sand, then lost her balance. Steve caught her and pulled her up.

"You should have let me help you," he said while she slapped sand off her knees.

Don't say it! Teddy warned herself. *Let the shadows work for you. Smile. Say, "Guess so."*

She took a step and nearly fell again. The awkward terrain, the agony of wanting to be anywhere but where she was, the aching delight in being right here, right now, with Steve Maloney. . . . So foreign, so frightening she hadn't initially felt the throb in her ankle.

"You okay?"

"Uh . . . yeah. Ow!"

"You sure?"

"Yeah, come on." She started to walk and thought she was disguising her pain quite well.

"Howie said you were a tough broad. Guess he was right. Most girls would want me to carry 'em."

Was that a trace of admiration in his voice or mocking? Teddy decided to keep walking.

"Guess Howie was right," Steve mumbled as he caught up with her.

A gust of wind blew them closer as they followed the small dot of light from Steve's flashlight. The dot led them up and out of the sand and into the high whip grass. The grass swayed in breathy wisps to and fro, graceful and elegant in the fingers of the wind.

"This way," Steve said, leading Teddy through the grass.

He led her up a knoll where the gnarled, low pines claimed the hillside. "There's a path along the ridge."

But with the path, with the pines, came darkness.

"Hope that flashlight holds out," Teddy said.

Steve stopped and put the light under his chin, giving his handsome face a monstrous distortion. "Why? You afraid of the dark?"

If Howie had been pulling this stunt, Teddy would have seized the flashlight and thrown it into the woods beyond, displaying her superior courage in the foreign darkness. Instead, she cautiously replied, "No, but I don't know the path."

"Come on. Let's take a breather."

They left the path where a huge old pine kept watch over the beach. Steve sat down and leaned against the trunk.

118

"Come on, Teddy. It's dry here. Have a seat."

"Maybe I ought to be getting back."

"What for? It's early. Take a load off." He turned off the flashlight and pointed toward the rocks offshore. "Great view." Teddy sat next to him and looked out over the ocean. Pitch black.

"I can't see—"

"Wait," Steve interrupted with a whisper. Then, as their eyes adjusted and as the clouds whirled by, the moon cast an occasional glimpse of the silver surf. "There's your view."

He pulled out a flask, took a long slurp, then offered some to Teddy.

"You got the pain?"

"No, and I think I better keep it that way."

"Warms your innards," he replied. "Go ahead. Won't kill you."

She took a drink and didn't wince once as the whiskey snaked its fiery way down her throat. Tears came to her eyes, and she thanked God the clouds had once again taken away the moon. Steve smiled at her, and before she'd thought better of it, she smiled back.

"I got my bands off last spring," Steve said, taking another drink. He pulled out his cigarettes and lit one. "Ever use your bands to shoot spit wads?"

"Paper clips go farther," Teddy replied, her back starting to relax against the tree trunk.

Steve, middrink, sprayed out a mouthful of whiskey, coughed, laughed, coughed.

When he regained his breath, Teddy asked, "So, you fish, huh?"

"Yeah. With my dad. Got three older brothers in the war, so I gotta help out all I can."

"No kidding? They seeing any action?" Teddy'd heard the question asked so many times in the last three years, it seemed almost a courtesy.

"Two are. Don's pushing a pencil for Halsey in the South Pacific. Phil's somewhere in North Africa." He exhaled cigarette smoke, which lofted quickly away.

"What about the third?"

"That's Harry. Marines. He's . . . um . . . he's missing just now."

Teddy leaned forward and tried to catch as much of Steve's face as the night would allow. "Oh. Rough luck. How long's he been missing?"

"Oh, don't worry. He'll show up. Don't see where jungles are any thicker'n the woods in the back hills. Harry's the best woodsman I know. He's just hanging out somewhere, waiting the Japs out."

He took another drink and smiled, staring off toward the horizon. "I can just see him now. Walking down out of those hills, that shit-eating grin on his face . . . all fat on pig meat and bananas. Tan as hell. Couple of lady friends."

Teddy tried to see Steve's vision out on the ocean. "Sure. They say lots of guys can survive those jungles if they know about woods and all." She had no idea what she was talking about.

"Funny. Harry's my favorite. Wouldn't know it to watch us. Fought like cats and dogs." He took another drink. "You know how it is." He flicked his cigarette out over the dunes below.

"Yeah. Me and Howie fight."

Steve was now well on his way to slurring his speech. His face was less congenial. "Well, you oughta apologize, you know," he whispered.

"For what? I didn't do anything!"

"I mean . . . you never know when you won't get another chance."

"What? That's stupid. . . . Howie's—"

"No . . . no . . . no . . ." Steve interrupted. "Shhhh." He put his finger to her lips. "Listen to what I'm telling you. . . ."

Teddy was suddenly uncomfortable. Steve was clearly drunk, his manner changed, his face hard, his eyes vague and frightening.

"Poor old Bluebird . . ."

"I think I gotta be going, Steve."

"Here? Want the rest?" He offered her the flask, and she took it to keep him from drinking more.

He watched her sip, and his smile returned. Perhaps it was his smile, perhaps it was the whiskey, but Teddy relaxed again and asked, "So who's this poor old Bluebird?"

"Harry's bitch."

"That's it. I'm going . . . ," Teddy said, starting to rise.

"A bitch is a female dog, stupid," Steve said, pulling her back down.

"Oh. So if she's poor and old, that mean she's dead too?"

Steve nodded. "Ran over her with my truck."

All Teddy could envision was a flattened, cartoon version of her mother's holy terror, Perkie. "Gee. Too bad," she managed.

"Harry was home on leave last summer. Jeez, he looked solid . . . all tan and his uniform and everything." His smile faded, and he said, "I didn't even have the guts to 'fess up, let alone tell him I was sorry about Bluebird. Ever feel so goddamn bad about something you can't even talk about it?"

Teddy took another sip and mumbled, "So is Harry the type to hold a grudge?"

Steve smiled, and somehow Teddy knew Steve and Harry looked alike. "Nah," Steve whispered, "I don't think so. Doesn't matter. The first thing I gotta do when Harry gets back is tell him I killed Bluebird and I'm sorry. Sorrier'n anything I've done in my whole life," Steve continued. "Anything left in that?" He took the flask and tapped the last drop out.

"Well, he'll know it was an accident. I mean, it was an accident, wasn't it?" Teddy asked.

" 'Course it was an accident. What'd you think, I'd kill my brother's dog just for the fun of it?"

"I don't know what you'd do," Teddy said in defense of her casualness. After all, more than once she'd considered how pleasant life would be without that wretched Perkie.

Steve flipped on the flashlight, pulled out his wallet and mumbled, "Here, I'll show you something. Hold the light."

He finally found a slip of paper and, in the dim light, read aloud to Teddy. " 'Paid in Full. Pick of the litter. Harry L. Maloney.' See? Fifty bucks this cost me. Look here. 'Schaefer Kennels, Vernonia, Oregon.' Best line of weimaraners in the state."

"Bluebird must have been some dog."

"Yeah, but this'll set things straight." He paused and looked at Teddy. A slow smile, then, "Come on, you. Enough about dead dogs. Tide's coming in. Let's see how that damn dam of yours is holding up." He carefully returned the receipt to its keeping place and pulled Teddy to her feet.

They walked the rest of the way toward the stream in silence. He led, she followed.

When they were in front of Rose's, Teddy looked up cautiously. All she could see peeking out from the treetops was the widow's walk. A few steps farther and she could see Rose had turned off all but the front-porch and side-door lights.

"Think your old lady'll still be up?" Steve asked, swaying a little in the deep sand.

"She's not my old lady."

"So she's your old lady's old lady, which makes her an even older old lady. Think she's up and waiting for you?"

"Nah. Most of the lights are out. It doesn't matter anyway. She thinks my brother's protecting me. There's a laugh."

From there they followed the stream up toward the bridge. Only a faint offering came from the streetlight on the bridge, but it was enough to illuminate Teddy's dam below.

"There. You see? I warned you about the tides," Steve said, spotlighting serious damage on the dam.

Teddy took the flashlight and looked closer. "Damn it! The tide book said only a seven-foot tide!"

"And which way is the wind blowing?"

Teddy turned toward the ocean, and as though to punctuate Steve's point, a gust of warm, wet wind swooshed her back a step.

The ocean was high and foamy and surfing over the

stream. They had to move to accommodate the rising water.

"All my hard work!" Teddy howled, watching two planks race each other for the ocean. She jumped into the stream to save them.

"What the hell you doing?" Steve called out.

"I stole these fair 'n' square, and I'm not letting them go out to sea!" she called, flopping one plank on the shore and returning for the other that, by now, was much farther downstream.

By the time the second plank was rescued, both Steve and Teddy were soaking wet. Teddy thanked him for the help and for walking her home from the fort.

"Here. Take this, would you?" Steve asked, handing Teddy the flask. "My mom finds this, I'm dead. Besides, she's got enough to worry about what with Harry and Don and all."

"Why not just hide it?"

"Nah. You keep it, eh? Bring it back full next time, and I'll tell you what you're doing wrong on your dam." Steve was standing now, cold, wet, shivering, on the opposite shore of the stream. "Well . . . guess I better shag my hide on home," he called out. "Be seeing you."

"Yeah," Teddy returned, as loudly as she dared. "Be seeing you!"

SIXTEEN

JE122—*It's late, so I'll make this short. I met this boy—he's okay. Starting tonight I'm hiding this journal in a safer place. Probably somewhere in the attic. Howie'd just love to read this. P.S. I'm thinking about growing my hair longer.*

Keeping true to her promise of increased journal security, Teddy took to the attic the next day. The storm was still raging, and since the dam was all but destroyed, she decided to get to work on the attic.

Rose had taken Howie up to Astoria to buy him some foul-weather gear in preparation for his fishing, so the house was alone and empty, the way Teddy preferred for missions such as hers.

She took the flask Steve had entrusted to her care and, no time like the present, filled it from Rose's well-stocked liquor cabinet. This time: gin. She added some water to the bottle from which she stole, hoping Rose wouldn't notice. Then, journal and flask in hand, she ascended.

First and foremost, the widow's walk. The door, fat and swollen by the rain, took an extra shove to open. A few seagulls were frightened off their perches, insulted after so many years of widow's walk dominion.

Ignoring the rain, Teddy looked down on her dam through the telescope. Yesterday's engineering masterpiece was today merely a few rocks in formation . . . looking more like stepping-stones than a foundation. The high tides of the night before had left the stream misshapen and meandering. Its calm in the wake of such random destruction annoyed Teddy.

Looking like a field general gazing down upon the battle-field, Teddy mentally made notes: *Move it all up even closer to the bridge. Yes, the water's deeper there, but it's farther from the ocean. Yes, build a wall higher here, lower slope there . . . and for God's sake, take your time. Maybe Steve knows something about this stream. August first. Weeks away. Think about it. Take your time.*

This resolved, Teddy climbed back down into the attic and resumed her task. She began by stacking boxes so that walls, nearly four boxes high, were built around the large window seat that overlooked the ocean. After two hours' time, she'd nearly created an entire room within the attic. She unrolled an old carpet, swept as much dust out of it as she had patience to and placed it in the center. Two old tables, a ragged sofa, an ancient lamp, all deserving of the attic, were placed around. She stacked, restacked, dusted, coughed, tidied and swept.

When it was done, she sat on the old sofa, thanking God she wasn't allergic to the glittering dust particles sifting down like fog in February. As it settled and she surveyed

126

her new place, her eyes came to rest on the window seat. *Could use some pillows.* Rose, apparently unable to part with the past, must have them somewhere, simply awaiting resurrection.

If Rose was a pack rat, she was a well-organized one. All the boxes, crates and bags were identified in some manner. Sheets, blankets, blackout cloth, *Sunset Magazine*s, Aunt Emily's hats, sheet music, Nah Nah's ashes . . .

"Nah Nah's ashes?" Teddy asked out loud. Recoiling at the touch of the shoe box, she let it drop to the floor. Poorly packed, poor Nah Nah—a few ashes fluttered out as the box hit the floor.

Teddy looked down and froze, unsure of what to do. She blinked down, bit her lip and wondered if it was sacrilege to laugh. Using a crate for balance, she carefully took off her tennis shoe, where some of the coarse, gray silt had landed, and she carefully ushered the ashes back to their resting place in the shoe box. "Thousand pardons" was all she could think of to say. She resecured the lid and placed the box high and away. But there was a pronounced scrunch from under her other shoe as she turned. She slowly lifted her foot and saw a small speck of Nah Nah—ashes to ashes, dust to dust, to attic floorboards.

She repressed a shudder and the desire to laugh and went back to work looking for pillows. *That box there, under six others, has a very pillowy look about it,* Teddy thought. She lifted, restacked, paused for breath, and unearthed it.

"An-ti-ma-cass-ars?" Teddy asked the rafters overhead. "Now, who's she?" Teddy preferred not to find out.

But the box next to Aunti Macassars caught her eye. It

127

was large and taped securely, always an attraction. She pulled it out and into the center where the light was better. It appeared to be unopened. She dusted off the top and read the address label. It read:

```
Miss Theadora and Master Howard Ramsey
1334 E. Pershing
Tacoma, Washington


Do not open until Christmas!!
```

It was from Rose in Minneapolis. The postmark was December 10, 1935. Then, in big red letters across the top were the words: Refused—Return to Sender.

It was her mother's handwriting.

The knife was poised to slit the box open when a door slammed downstairs.

"Hey, Teddy? You up there?" Howie called out.

Teddy heard footsteps on the stairs and quickly shoved the box away, stacking something on top to hide her discovery. This was something she must have all to herself.

Howie arrived at the door just as Teddy was coming to meet him, scaring him so that he dropped the bags he was carrying.

"Damn it, don't do that!" he screeched. He took a moment to compose himself, then said, "Look at this stuff Rose bought me." He proceeded to pull out slickers, boots, gloves.

"Yeah, yeah. Look at this," she said, pulling him toward her new room.

He was impressed. "Jeez, neat. Talk about a storm fort!"

"No way, Howie. This is just for me. Maybe you, once in a while, but no one else. Got it?"

As she should have known they would, Howie's eyes quickly came to rest on the silvery flask Steve had entrusted to her care.

"And what is this?" he asked, opening it and whiffing its contents.

"Give it back!" Teddy growled, grabbing it.

"Hey, that's Steve's!"

"So what?"

"He give it to you?"

"Yeah. He didn't want his mom to find it."

That seemed to satisfy Howie as he walked around the room. Then, "You and him get along okay?"

"Yeah."

"You like him?"

"He's all right."

"He try anything?"

"Yeah, sure," Teddy answered sarcastically.

"He's made it with just about every girl in town, you know. And he still has another year of high school."

"Well, he didn't make it with me. Besides," she added, "he's just a friend."

Howie had completed his inspection of the room. He picked up the flask and pointed it at her. "I think you better keep it that way. And you better watch it drinking this stuff. Makes you do things you shouldn't ought to."

"Kids?" Rose's voice called up from downstairs. "Lunch."

Howie called back down, "Coming, Rose." Then he handed Teddy the flask and gathered up his packages.

129

"How about you, Howie?" Teddy asked carefully. "You make it with anyone yet?"

Howie grinned at her. "Maybe I have and maybe I haven't."

"What? You don't know?"

"Howie? Teddy?"

"Right there, Rose!" Teddy called from the top of the stairs. True confessions could wait. She walked past her brother, poked him in the stomach and said, "Come on, Casanova. Lunch." And she led him down the stairs. Down, away from the box, away from the mystery it must surely hold.

SEVENTEEN

Teddy tossed in bed that night, unable to hold a dream. The unopened box upstairs called to her, even though she had promised herself it must wait until she was once again alone in the house. But her eyes refused the offer of sleep, and she stared at the ceiling.

She waited another hour, then crept to her door and carefully opened it. No light was escaping from under Howie's or Rose's door. It was safe.

Her aching curiosity was far greater than her fear of the dark house. She dared not turn on any lights for fear of being discovered. The last staircase up was the darkest, closed at top and bottom. But she climbed slowly until her outstretched hands felt the attic door. She opened it and stepped through. Slowly, her eyes adjusted to the gloom and she could see enough to find the light switch.

Her attic fort at night seemed far smaller than in the daylight. Ignoring the rising tide of fear of things hiding here, eyes piercing there, tiny specs of Nah Nah among the

131

floorboards, she went straight to the unopened Christmas box. Slowly, quietly, she pulled it into her lair, took the knife and slit the crusted packing tape.

She opened the top and went through wads and wads of crumpled newspaper. Then, very much like a child on Christmas morning, she pulled out the first treasures. Dresses. Two. One red, one blue. Lovely little things. She held them up. Perfect fit, for a six-year-old. The card attached read, "To a lovely little girl, Theadora. From Grandma Dumont."

Then a cowboy outfit, complete with holsters and guns. "To my little cowboy, Howard. From Grandma Dumont."

Digging deeper, Teddy pulled out two stuffed animals of unknown species. No need to look at the cards—one for each twin.

Teddy reached in deeper still. This time, a doll. Two feet high, it must have been. Sweet, curly black hair, flawless smiling face, perfect little dimpled hands. But Teddy had despised dolls all her life. They were for other little girls, not her.

A creak on the steps startled Teddy, and by reflex she stashed all the gifts back into the box, being sure to place the doll at the very bottom. She listened for further trespass but only heard her heart stampeding in her chest. Then, again the sound from below. She was at the attic door to head him off. It was Howie, damn him! Nothing was sacred to that creep!

"I *knew* I'd find you up here," he said as he entered.

"Get out of here, Howie! I told you, this is *my* place!"

"You don't own it."

"I'm warning you . . ."

Howie waltzed past his sister and entered her domain. Seeing the box, he said, "Aha! Snooping! Always snooping!"

"Look, what d' you want, Howie?" Teddy asked, stepping between the box and her brother.

"Find anything good?" he asked, going around her and looking at the box. "What's in that?"

"Nothing. Just old stuff of Rose's."

"Come on, show me," Howie said, circling the box. Then his eyes came to rest on the address label. "Hey, that's us on the box."

Too late and useless. Teddy opened the box and pulled out the cowboy suit. "Here. Merry Christmas from Rose," she announced flatly.

Howie held the suit up to him and fingered the small, leather-trimmed hat. "Huh?"

"Yeah, all of it. Christmas shit Rose sent to us. Look at the postmark—hell, this stuff . . ."

Howie looked into the box and said, "I don't get it."

"Neither did we. Look, you idiot, Mom refused this stuff. Wouldn't even open it. There's probably a box just like this around here somewhere from every Christmas since . . ."

Howie sank to his knees and said, ". . . Since the fire?"

Teddy nodded.

"Mom must have had a good reason," Howie said. "I mean, why'd she keep all this stuff from us when we were so god-awful poor?"

"Rose didn't come," Teddy said, taking the cowboy suit and gently packing it away.

Howie had perched in the window seat, and as he spoke, he looked out over the blackness of the night. "You know, I try and I try. I'll be damned if I can remember—"

Teddy cut him off. "We were only four."

"Yeah, but *you* remember. How come I don't?"

"I'm smarter."

"Screw you."

Teddy pulled the box into the shadows where it belonged and joined Howie. "Guess tomorrow we oughta do those swim lessons. . . ."

"Tell me again what happened." Howie looked at his sister in the window's reflection.

"I teach you to swim, you give me twenty-five percent. God, you're dumb!"

Howie faced his sister and repeated, "Tell me again what happened, Teddy."

"Look, a million times I told you . . . the Christmas tree caught on fire. The house burned down."

"Daddy and Francesca—"

"They died, goddamn it, Howie! You know all this!"

"Daddy grabbed us . . ."

"Yeah, yeah, he got us and Mom, then went back for the baby. . . ."

"I can't remember," Howie whispered to the night.

"You don't have to. Look, it's late."

Howie never pressed past Francesca, but just to make sure he didn't, Teddy baited him with, "There's a dead person up here."

"Go to hell."

"No, I mean it. Wanna see?"

"You're full of shit."

She rose and smiled enticingly at him. "Wanna see?"

"What do you mean a dead person . . . what, a body?"

He followed his sister as she pulled out the shoe box full of Nah Nah Stokes.

She opened the lid, held it for Howie to behold and said, "Howie, meet Nah Nah Stokes—Nah Nah, meet Howie."

Howie stared into the box of gray, his face a color to match.

Teddy put her ear to the box and said, "What was that? Oh. Sure." Then, to Howie, "She says, 'Howjewdo?' "

"Huh?"

"Look, ashes, you dope. Nah Nah Stokes's ashes."

"That's just sand. Isn't it?" He took a closer look and recoiled appropriately. Teddy grinned at his horror.

"Put it away!" he yelled.

Unable to pass it up, she shoved the box under his face.

"I mean it, Teddy! Get it out of here!"

Teddy might normally have been tempted to tease him beyond his limit. Perhaps it was the terror in his eyes, the shrillness of his voice . . . she put the lid on the shoe box and set it down.

"Just thought you two ought to meet, that's all," she said, with a hint of Boris Karloff in her voice.

"Screw you," Howie said, looking around the room. Then, "Hey, where're my *National Geographic*s? You didn't toss 'em, did you?"

"They're out there, behind that sofa."

Howie rummaged through the stack, found one and tucked it into his bathrobe.

"Yeah, guess we'd better do swim lessons tomorrow," he said.

Howie left the attic, and Teddy felt like screaming so loudly the entire town would think the Japs were bombing.

It was late, but there was time for one journal entry:

JE123—Howie drives me over-the-top crazy! Get this: he's afraid of Nah Nah's ashes. Howard the Coward strikes again. What a sissy. He was trying to remember the fire again. I had to get his attention. Nah Nah worked just swell.

You know, I don't know what will come first: Howard the Coward will finally remember how it really was and go crazy, or I'll go crazy and tell him myself and then we'll all be crazy.

EIGHTEEN

Five weeks passed in relative harmony. As promised, Teddy taught Howie how to swim with minimal embarrassment and no drowning. So Howie went fishing on the Maloney boat. Naturally, their mother had to be placated with the promise that Howie wouldn't get too close to the boat's sides. As it turned out, teaching Howie how to swim was the smartest move Teddy had made: she got him out of her hair for long stretches of time, and when he returned, he had cash, twenty-five percent of which she received as payment for the lessons and the accompanying silence. And Teddy had the beach, the stream, the house and Rose to herself.

Teddy and Rose had become fast friends. They did mother-daughter things she and her mom had never ventured—shopped, saw movies, bowled, played rousing matches of double solitaire, laughed. Somehow, it was all so easy with Rose, who never once asked Teddy to wear gloves or suggested just a smidge of foundation to blend the freckles. It was even Rose's suggestion that the yellowsashed dress, gloves, anklets, and Mary Janes be donated away out of her life and into the life of some needy war orphan.

Best summer ever, Teddy admitted to her journal. Only occasionally, only on Sundays when they called, did Dee Dee cross Teddy's mind.

The July weather was glorious. The storm fort was called into duty only a handful of times since that first night Teddy had visited. Parties now were on the beach, proud and daring in the open air, where summer parties should be, where the huge bonfire could attract other kids, summer kids. New faces, new challenges, new temptations.

Since that first summer storm had claimed the beginnings of Teddy's dam, she had become much wiser about the next step. Now she consulted not only the tide book, but the weather forecast as well. She spent days combing the beach for planks of great strength and will. She built her stockpile up toward the house so that other "thieves" wouldn't carry off her plunder. She rolled countless rocks from both sides of the stream. Since Steve had not even mentioned his dam or the bet or the deadline, Teddy had no shame about "stealing" from his side of the stream. Her stockpile of stones stacked in the sand resembled miniature pyramids of Egypt. When she wasn't gathering and rolling, she was sitting and staring at the stream and thinking engineering thoughts.

It was now eleven days until August first. Long-range forecasts looked great, tides shouldn't be a problem. She'd begin on Saturday, the twenty-ninth. Plenty of time.

Teddy had spent her late afternoons away from the stinging sun, perfecting her attic, stacking and snooping, even oiling the telescope so that it swiveled a full 360 degrees. Rose held true to her threat and had an electrician inspect the wiring. She also held true to her promise not to set foot in the attic until Teddy deemed it ready. When that time came, Teddy led Rose upstairs with an excitement she hadn't felt since she was a child. Rose was duly impressed. Teddy offered tea prepared with unearthed treasures: an old hot plate, a tea set, linen napkins.

Their talk had been light, just a regular tea party. Then, when it looked as though Rose was ready to descend into the house, Teddy pulled out the shoe box, Nah Nah's, from behind the sofa. She'd wrapped it in a red ribbon for the presentation. Thinking she was offering Rose something years ago lost, she was startled by Rose's reaction.

"And just where did you find this?" she snapped, grabbing the box.

"Uh . . . well, hiding over there somewhere. I thought maybe you lost it or—"

"Well, you thought wrong! I wanted it hidden!"

Never before had Teddy seen Rose's face so flushed, her words so harsh. She held the box to her chest.

"I'm sorry, Rose. I'll put it back," Teddy offered, holding her hands out for the box.

But Rose sank onto the sofa, looking at the box now in her lap. Her face softened, and she said, "It was always so hot up here. Since she put me through such hell, I thought she'd feel right at home in the heat up here."

"Did she ever request what, you know, you should do with . . . the ashes?" Teddy asked carefully.

"She requested the waters of Tahiti," Rose said. "But she only deserves the attic."

Teddy felt safe in asking, "A holy terror?"

"Oh yes," Rose answered, a smile on her face.

"Then I guess you won't mind that I spilled a little of her," Teddy confessed sheepishly.

Rose threw her head back and laughed her gutsy laugh, the one Teddy had come to know and love and imitate.

"I sort of crunched some of her into the floorboards," Teddy added, pointing to the corner. "By accident, of course."

Rose laughed louder.

"I couldn't get her all up."

Rose now had tears spilling from her eyes as she laughed. Teddy was afraid the entire box would slip off her lap and the hilarity of that might send Rose into apoplexy.

"I guess that means I'll have a little bit of ol' Nah Nah over my head forever! God, she'd love that."

Teddy laughed with her grandmother, although, for the life of her, she wasn't convinced it was all that funny.

"Here, Rose," Teddy said, going for the box. "I'll hide her good, once and for all. . . ."

But, calming herself, Rose replied, "No, no. I'll take Nah Nah down with me."

Teddy let her leave. She hadn't had the courage to bring up the issue of old, unopened Christmas boxes. She certainly wasn't going to mention it now. Not after Nah Nah. Things were going too well for Teddy to start meddling with anything else in their family's past.

Teddy spent her early evenings on the beach forming cautious friendships in the most forgiving, ebbing light of the setting sun and the building fire. Her freckles at last had surrendered to the sun, and she now looked tanned and robust, rather than spotted. If anyone noticed this gradual change, they didn't mention it.

She always left the parties early before the guitar, before the pairing, before the partying, for she had other things to do. She'd enjoy late evenings after the house was quiet. . . . Rose out doing her war work or in bed with a book, Howie on the beach discovering God-knows-what. She'd listen to music, read, occasionally play the piano, spy from the widow's walk. Or sometimes, late and alone, she would sit in the window seat, writing in her journal.

Things were fine in Teddy's life . . . Howie out, Rose in, Steve somewhere in between, her mother a two-day drive away, money in the bank, an attic for her thoughts, and the Best Damn Dam of 1944 nearly in her pocket.

One late afternoon, Teddy sat on the widow's walk, a glass of lemonade at her side, feet propped up, journal in her lap. The horizon clouds forecast a sunset of petulant pinks and glorious golds. Crows insulted seagulls, a warm breeze seduced the treetops and all was well with the world.

Teddy surveyed her domain: the stream, the ocean, the town, the bridge, the street. She strolled around the walk, and her eyes came to rest on a large truck coming through town. It struck her odd that a hay truck should come rambling through town. Oh, of course, there were stables somewhere around. She guessed even weathered old beach nags couldn't live on seaweed. But the truck didn't take Seaview south. Instead, it turned down their street.

It came closer, high-stacked bales challenging the low treetops along their lane. *Clearly lost*, she thought. She whirled the telescope around and brought the truck into its scope. The glare off the window's reflection made it impossible to tell . . . oh God, wait a minute. . . . Teddy focused closer and saw the passenger. Her face hardened. She took the glass of lemonade and heaved it into the treetops, and with it, she screamed, "God damn it all to hell!"

Dee Dee the Divine, Dee Dee the Delish, Dee Dee the Deluxe was back . . . unannounced, unauthorized and unwelcome.

There was something painfully discordant in Dee Dee's high-pitched "yoooo hoooo" and the deep, lopsided diesel toot of the truck's horn, all to the accompaniment of Perkie's falsetto yapping.

Rose finally came out and stood, hands on hips, unbelieving and looking every inch like Rose of the Beach, not Rose of the Wig, Rose of the Rouge, Rose of the Past. Teddy crouched down to watch the reunion, wondering how many days she could last on the widow's walk before they rooted her out.

She watched the trucker climb out of the cab. He walked around and, with great arms, lifted Dee Dee down. Dee Dee made a fetching, delicate cargo. He set her down, gently lifted Perkie down and together—the mother, the trucker, the dog—they approached Rose. Teddy watched them through the telescope. There was no need to hear the words. Their faces said it all. Dee Dee: speechless, shocked, accessorized. Rose: cordial, cool, pissed. Driver: sorry he'd come.

NINETEEN

Like that very first day, Teddy didn't have the desire, the grace or the guts to face any of them just yet. Neither simple good manners nor grating curiosity could make her attempt the living room. She took the stairs down and listened before opening the door. She heard Howie's voice embrace their mother. Quietly, carefully, for she knew Howie would be listening for her escape, she continued down to the basement. She surfaced safely outside, keeping as far away from their voices as she could.

As she walked their lane, circling the hay truck with disgust, she silently cursed her mother for what was, to date, her most obvious attempt to ruin Teddy's life. So, to hell with surprise visits. Let Rose handle it. If she stayed away long enough, maybe chili and beer would come to the rescue. That was it. Let them all get slightly waxed, then she could casually appear, sober and in charge.

She knew she had to be out of calling distance, out of the range of the brass bell. So she allowed the northern breeze to usher her south, south toward California, Mexico, Tierra del Fuego, south to the storm fort.

She crawled in and was at once comforted by the now familiar and healing aroma of burned, salted wood. She easily forgave the musty odors and the stale light. The sand into which she plopped welcomed her with cool, accommodating comfort. She played with the sand, allowing handfuls to drift slowly between her fingers. How odd, no matter how tightly she grasped a handful of sand, it still leaked out . . . maybe only a few grains here and there, but eventually, she lost the entire handful. The tighter the grasp, the faster the loss.

She knew she was surrounded by hidden caches of booze, bottles and flasks dug into the hillside, awaiting resurrection for the next party. The cave almost echoed Steve's holy chant, borrowed from his idolized Harry, "Who's got the pain? Who's got the pain?" Echoing back, the correct answer, "I do, I do."

She unrolled a blanket, pulled it around herself and found it easy to fall asleep to the invisible chanting, the ocean's steady roar and the wind singing through the blanket entrance.

"I *knew* I'd find you here!" Howie barked, kicking Teddy awake. "Get on home!"

"You're not the boss of me," Teddy growled back, pulling her head under the blanket. Stupid, infantile thing to say, fresh out of their toddlerhood.

"Mom said."

"She's not the boss of me either."

"You're acting like an asshole!" Howie pursued.

"Get lost."

"You been drinking?"

"No."

"You show up drunk, and Mom'll kill you!"

"You think I'd be stupid enough to drink when Mom's around? She'd never live through it. I'd kill her with honesty." Teddy sat up and stared coldly at her brother, who was digging for a bottle. "That goes for you too, Howie," she added, pulling him away from the cave wall.

Howie sat down and threw some pebbles at the rug door. *Ping! Ping!* they hit, ricocheting nicely back. "God, Teddy, he's about the stupidest man I've ever met!"

"Who is he, anyway? Hey! Stop that, will you? You hit me."

Howie leaned back and stared at the rooted ceiling. "A truck driver, for God's sake. Sid. Even his name is stupid. Sid."

"What's she come for?" Teddy asked, barely audible.

"Take a guess. To get our approval, that's why. I mean it, Teddy, the guy can barely form words!"

"Approval? What for? They getting married?" Teddy asked, with absolutely no feelings one way or another at such a sudden prospect.

Howie rolled over and looked at his sister. His face was square with a slow-to-surface handsomeness, his eyes were intense and honest, yet his voice was still boyish, innocent, angry as he said, "They already are. She married the jerk. Just met him and she married him. No asking us first, no nothing. Like we don't exist."

"You bullshitting me, Howard?" Teddy demanded, grabbing his arm.

But his eyes, now tear-laden, told her he wasn't bullshit-

145

ting. "Mom married a pickup, plain and simple. Ever hear anything so cheap?"

Teddy stared at her brother in disbelief. Her calling their mother cheap was one thing, Howie calling her cheap was another. This might be more trouble than the whole affair was worth, but she ventured, "Jeez, Howie, I wouldn't exactly call her cheap."

"You wouldn't? What would you call someone whose car breaks down and some trucker comes along and, what, four weeks later they're married? What would you call a woman like that?"

"Well, I don't know why you're so shocked. Didn't I tell you that was what Mom was going to do all along? Get us out of her hair long enough to snag someone?"

Howie had the look of a kid who, for the first time, had conquered multiplying fractions. "That's right. You called it. Cripes, did you ever."

"So, does she expect us to come home with her?" Teddy asked cautiously.

"I didn't stick around long enough to find out. Who cares what Mom wants, anyway? I've got a job, and I'm staying down here. She and that stupid-ass Sid jerk can take a flying leap for all I care, I'm . . ."

Teddy stared at her brother in disbelief. "Look, Rose'll make it right. She'll talk Mom into letting us stay," she assured him.

"Oh, Rose! That's another thing! She talked nice and friendly, but I could tell, looking at her, she's fit to be tied."

"Maybe we ought to be getting back. Poor Rose. I didn't think about her up against Dee Dee and that guy all alone." Teddy got up and offered her hand to help Howie up.

"All right, now here's the plan," Howie began, leading the way back toward Rose's. "You and me stand together on this, you got it? We want to stay down here with Rose."

"Right. Maybe even right up to school starting," Teddy agreed.

Howie stopped, faced his sister and said firmly, "No, Teddy. We want to stay down here forever."

"You do? Want to stay down forever?" she asked.

"Now I do. No idiot truck driver is having a say in my life. Mom or no Mom. Uh-uh. Not this boy. I got plans here. I'm staying."

He took off at a determined pace, never hearing Teddy's response, which was, "Well, I'll be damned. Good for you, Howard."

TWENTY

Perkie the Pekingese announced their arrival. Teddy and Howie paused at the kitchen door, and before going inside, Howie reminded Teddy, "Honor Bright? We want to stay here."

"Got it."

"Teddy!" Howie snapped.

"Oh, all right, you stooge, Honor Bright! Come on, let's get this over with." And she pushed her way past him.

They appeared together at the doorway. Teddy stepped into the living room and shot a quick glance at Rose, who was sitting on the piano bench, beer in hand. Rose smiled, but Teddy couldn't read it from the distance.

"Oh, Theadorrrrraaaaa," Dee Dee gushed, putting down her beer and rushing toward her daughter. "Did you miss me? I missed you so much. Come on in here. There's someone very special I want you to meet."

The trucker stood up, and it seemed to Teddy as though he took up half the living room. He came forward, smiled and offered his hand as Dee Dee announced, "Theadora, this is Sidney Spirk, your new father. Sid, Theadora."

Teddy tried to get by with a nod, but Dee Dee added, "Now, I've already told Sid about your hands, so go ahead, shake."

Teddy shook hands with Sid and noticed how soft and warm his were considering his size and the awkward agony of the moment. He smiled down kindly at her and said, "Your mother tells me you play the piano."

"Some," Teddy mumbled. His eyes were large and blue, his hair blond and graying, his face simple and friendly.

"Maybe later you'll play for us, huh, Theadora?" Dee Dee continued, lighting a cigarette.

"So, you and him got married," Teddy began, casting her suspicious eye toward her brother, who was still leaning in the doorway.

Dee Dee took Sid's hand, and as they stood, looking into each other's adoring eyes, Teddy noticed a glint of something new in her mother's face. Oh, it was the same face of pastel perfection, but what had she added? Serenity, perhaps?

"Oh now, I know it's all rush-rush and everything, but come on, kids, give your poor mother a break, huh? Sid's swell, he really is."

"Well, you might at least have mentioned it on Sunday when we called," Howie said.

A chilly breeze of silence wafted through the room, and it was Rose who broke it with, "Now, listen, all of you. There isn't going to be any arguing over this. Sid, I'm sure my daughter warned you about all of us. Norman Rockwell has never called asking us to sit for him. Delores, now you've sprung a big one, and we're all going to have to get used to it."

"I wanted to surprise you," Dee Dee defended.

"Look, Deed," Sid began, "I think I'll take Perkie out for a walk."

In his discomfort, he didn't await a reply but struggled to leash Perkie, who firmly wanted to stay with Dee Dee.

"Wonk her on her rear," Teddy said. "Works for me."

He did, Perkie agreed and they left.

"So, what's the plan?" Teddy asked her mother.

"Well, I thought, after you and Rose get cleaned up some, Sid and I would take us all out to dinner. Someplace nice."

"No, I mean, you down here to take us back home, or what?"

"You can forget that, Mom!" Howie broke in. "I don't want anything to do with that monkey. I'm staying here. With Rose. Until graduation."

"You are?" Rose asked.

"It's okay, isn't it?"

"I suppose this is all your idea!" Dee Dee said curtly to Teddy.

"Well—" Teddy began, looking back at her mother.

"What do you mean you want to stay here?" Dee Dee boomed, cutting Teddy off. "You're both coming home with me and Sid and when I say!"

"Now, Dee Dee," Rose said, "there's plenty of time to hash this out."

"But we don't want to come home, Mom!" Howie yelled back. "You've got *him* now. What do you need us for?"

"What have you been poisoning their heads with, huh,

Mama?" Dee Dee asked, pointing her cigarette at her mother.

"Now, just you wait a minute, Delores . . . ," Rose began, raising her voice. "How were any of us to know you were going to come waltzing in here with a hay truck and a husband? Don't you think you might have prepared us a little? You can't blame the kids for acting shocked and hurt. Frankly, I'm a little shocked and hurt myself."

"Why? That I finally found myself a little happiness? Found myself a future? I'll have you know Sid *owns* that hay truck out there."

"Ever hear of an engagement or even just wedding invitations, Mom?" Howie demanded righteously.

"Don't you raise your voice to me, Howard!"

Rose approached her daughter and said, "He's right. Maybe something in the way of a small family gathering would have been called for."

"Really, Mama? Well, I doubt you would have come for that, either! I mean, since when have you ever been around when I needed you?" Dee Dee snapped back. Then came the tears. Teddy actually was proud of her mother for holding out as long as she had. Dee Dee slumped into a chair and fumbled through her purse for a hankie. "Oh, this isn't the way I'd planned this," she sobbed. "I thought you'd all be so happy for me, for us, for all of us."

"Mom, you've only known him for a few crummy weeks!" Howie hollered, unable to hold back any longer. "For ten years you've been a widow and then, *bam!* In a few lousy weeks you meet this Sid joker and marry him! What the hell were you thinking about?"

Dee Dee stopped crying and rose regally. With one very

deliberate, dramatic swipe, she slapped Howie across the face.

"I was thinking about me, for once," she said. She turned to Teddy and said, "Anything smart you want to add?"

Teddy paused before answering. She looked at Howie, whose shocked, stinging anger said it all. Of all the things she wanted to say, was tempted to say, she simply said, "You and your husband can have my room. I'll sleep in the attic." She turned and pulled Howie away. "Come on, Howie. Help me move my junk."

Howie remained silent until they arrived in the attic with a load of Teddy's things.

"I should have hit her back" was all he said as he threw a load of clothes down on the floor.

Teddy looked at Howie and knew their mother had hurt him. She touched her own face, and she could almost feel the sting and humiliation Howie felt. "I thought of smacking her myself," she replied. "But no telling what that Sid might have done if he found out."

"I don't care. I'd kill him if he ever touched us," he growled, swallowing tears.

"Yeah, but Mom would *still* be married to him."

"What the hell is that supposed to mean?"

"It means, Howie," Teddy said, losing her patience, "it means, you better cool the whole thing over. Mom loses you, she'll go nuts."

"What?"

"You know the sun rises and sets on you, Howie. It always has. If she doesn't get your approval of Sid, she'll make life miserable for everyone. Think about it."

152

"I don't care. I'll never forgive her for this," he said, opening the window seat.

"Hey, stay out of there."

"Where's Steve's flask? I want a drink."

"Don't be an idiot. I mean it, Howie. That's my stuff." They struggled over the window seat and its contents. Howie found the flask and won it in a vague tug-of-war with Teddy.

"Don't, Howie," she pleaded. "It'll only make matters worse."

He unscrewed the lid. He smiled his summer smile, the one fresh off the face of Steve Maloney. "Hey, I got the pain."

JE124—Well, Mom did it to us again. Just when things were going swell, for both Howie and me. If only she'd stay out of our lives long enough for things to get to normal, we might be a family once in a while. I guess that's stupid. I think Howie has a point. Maybe we could stay down here, go to school. Nah. She'd never let us. Howie's doing it all wrong. Me, I'm going to ride this one out. Give the jerk a chance. Sid. Heck, I think I even sort of like him. He's harmless.

Jeez, how am I going to get Howie back down to earth? Mom and Sid are leaving tomorrow to deliver that hay. Once they're gone, maybe Rose and me can figure something out. But oh God, they'll be back. One thing's for sure: Howie and me got to stick together on this. This is the one time we got to be Siamese. And just as soon as he sobers up, I'll attach him.

TWENTY-ONE

The next morning, Teddy descended from the attic early, four-thirty, only slightly stiff from being a few inches longer than the couch on which she slept. Howie was in the kitchen, slumping over a cup of coffee. Teddy could feel the vibrations from his throbbing head across the room.

"You alive?"

"Shiiiiit . . . ," he whispered back, not turning his head.

"You drank that whole flask?"

"Shiiiiit . . ."

Teddy poured herself a cup of coffee and asked, "Where's Rose?"

"Not up yet."

"Who made the coffee?"

"I thought you did."

"No, I just woke up."

Howie's hand shook as he lifted the cup to his lips. "Why you up so early?"

"I got to go to the bathroom."

"Flush quietly, will you?"

When Teddy came back, she wasn't surprised to see that her brother hadn't moved an eyelash in her absence. "I don't think you're in any shape to go fishing, Howie."

"Well, I ain't in any shape to stay around here today." Teddy's nose guided her to the oven, and she opened the door to nearly risen biscuits. "Ummmm," she said as she sniffed. "Rose must be up, Howie. Those sure as death aren't Mom's biscuits."

"Christ, who cares? I'm not eating anything, anyway."

Teddy sat down across from Howie and watched his agony. Under normal circumstances, she would have teased him, crashed around a little, anything to irritate him.

"You know, Howie, I was thinking—"

"I don't want to hear it!" he snapped. "Just leave me alone."

She pulled his hand away from his eyes and said, "Well, you *are* going to hear it!"

But they were both interrupted by a creaking coming from the dining room. "Shut up!" Howie growled. "Rose is coming!"

But it wasn't Rose, nor was it Dee Dee. It was Sid, apron around his waist, smile on his face, coffee cup in his hand, who appeared before them.

"Timer go off yet?" he asked, muffing his hand and opening the oven. He pulled out the biscuits, gave them an eye of approval and placed the pan on the stove top. He turned to the stunned twins and asked, "How do you like your eggs?"

"Scrambled," Teddy replied warily. "Where's Rose?"

"The girls were up late. How about you, Howie? Scrambled?"

Howie just turned back toward his coffee.

"How about it, buddy? A man needs a good breakfast before heading out for a day fishin'," Sid continued, whisking up Teddy's eggs.

Howie rose and nearly tipped his chair in his haste. "I'm not your buddy, I don't want any breakfast and you know where you can stuff those biscuits!"

He stomped out of the kitchen. Sid's face reddened, but not with an angry red, more an embarrassed red. Teddy wished she'd stayed upstairs and used the couch-side pee-bucket.

Sid continued whisking the eggs and slapped a scoop of bacon grease into the cast-iron skillet. Teddy knew she should say something, so she offered, "Howie's not himself lately."

The grease sizzled and foamed, and Sid replied, "Your mother said you'd be the tough one."

The honesty of his statement caught Teddy off guard. "I've dedicated my life to proving my mother wrong." *There. That should test him. Maybe he can cook, but can he take heat? Might as well get used to it here and now.*

He kept on scrambling the eggs and said, "It runs in the family. They fought till midnight."

"So you pulled yourself out of bed in the middle of the night to cook biscuits and set us all straight, eh?" It was never too early in the morning for Teddy's sarcasm.

He turned and looked at her. "I just want to live through this." He smiled gently, then went back to his scrambling. No fighter he.

"Then let me give you a piece of advice, Sid. You can come between me and Mom, you can come between Howie

156

and Mom, but I swear to God, don't ever try to come between Howie and me. I'm the only one who understands
him. He doesn't need a father, and he doesn't need a
brother."

Sid listened as he served up two plates of biscuits and
eggs. He brought the plates to the table, sat down and
asked, "Tabasco?"

She handed it to him and added, "And another thing."

"I'm listening," he said, devouring his breakfast.

"Stay the hell out of our past."

He chewed thoughtfully, swallowed and replied, "You
stay out of mine, and I'll stay out of yours."

"Fair enough," Teddy said, slathering a biscuit with
honey. There was something so forthright about his words
and his manner that Teddy couldn't help liking him. And
his biscuits weren't bad, either.

Howie waited outside for Steve to pick him up for the
day's fishing. Teddy went back to her attic and waited for
the rest of the household to come to life. She vaguely heard
the phone ring downstairs. Odd, at five-thirty. Maybe the
fog bank wasn't going to accommodate fishing that morning. She heard Sid call outside to Howie. A door slammed.
The sound of Howie's bedroom door slamming below her
confirmed her analysis. Poor Howie. Now he was going to
have to face things head-on. A good day for dam building,
perhaps. *Sure, that's it. Take Howie down to the beach, give
him a shovel, put him to work.*

It was amazing to Teddy's way of thinking: her mother
and Rose, how they never seemed to acknowledge the argu-

ments of the night before, as though each granted silent forgiveness. No mention of anything. Just polite chitchat. It was quite a gift, actually. Thank God, she hadn't inherited it.

She crept into Howie's room and sat on his bed. The extra hours of sleep brought color to his face, and Teddy hesitated to wake him. His eyes still closed, he mumbled, "What do you want?"

"Let's hit the beach."

"They left yet?"

"God, your breath could knock a buzzard off a shit wagon."

"Then don't breathe."

"Come on, Howie. Haul it out."

"Not until they're gone."

"Come on. I need help with the dam."

"Where are they?"

"They went for a walk. The coast is clear."

"Not if they're on it."

"They're leaving after their walk. Look, you know Mom will come up here to kiss you goodbye. At least on the beach you can see her coming and vanish."

Howie opened his eyes and doubled his pillow to look at Teddy. "Something's wrong at Steve's."

"What d' you mean?"

"That was one of the crew who called me. They said the Maloney boat wouldn't be going out for a while. Family emergency or something. Shit, wouldn't you just know it? That job's the only thing letting me stay here, and now, nothing."

"Look, let's just get *them* out of town. Then we'll have some time to figure things out."

"I mean it, Teddy. I'm staying in Holiday."

"After they're gone, you, me and Rose will come up with something."

"If I have to enlist, I'm not going home."

"Ha! Enlist in what, the Junior Commandos?"

Teddy walked to the door, then added, "I'll be down at the stream. If you were smart, you'd come down there too."

Howie sat up in bed and his hands went to his head. "Jeeeeezzzzz."

"It's like I told you, creep. Mom ain't worth the hangover. When are you going to figure that out?" Teddy said cruelly.

Howie looked at her and replied, "I think I just did."

"Finally. Bring a shovel."

TWENTY-TWO

Dee Dee and Sid vanished as swiftly, as brazenly, as they had come. Hay truck and all. Complete with exit hugs, Dee Dee waving Perkie-paws bye-bye and Sid honking the truck's disturbing horn. Off and on their way south where Tillamook cows awaited their cargo.

Instead of saying goodbye, Howie opted for staying upstairs, in the bathroom, throwing up. Teddy had the grit to stand at Rose's side, waving.

As the truck vanished, Teddy asked, "Well?"

"He makes your mother happy, and that's all that matters."

"Howie hates him." Teddy could tell Rose's eyes had lost some of their sparkle. Today they were almost as flat as they had been on that first day of the silly red-wig masquerade.

Rose put her arm around Teddy and simply replied, "Your mother could have married Charles Lindbergh, John Wayne, *and* Douglas MacArthur, and Howie'd still hate him. He's the son. It's his job. He'll come around."

"Sid's kind of . . . slow, don't you think?"

"I don't think Dee Dee was looking for a mental challenge. Look, he makes her happy. . . ."

"Yeah, I guess."

The truck issued a final, faraway, farewell toot as it chugged through town. Rose added, "She's been needing him for a long time."

"Mind if I ask you something?" Teddy asked, watching Rose snatch up some weeds at the edge of the Victory garden.

"Shoot."

"Might be personal."

"Still shoot."

"When you came that one time, Howie and me were six, I guess . . . what happened?"

Rose kept plucking weeds, but asked back, "What do you remember?"

"Just you and Mom fighting on the front walk." Teddy pulled some weeds while she talked.

"Ever ask your mom what we were fighting about?"

"Mom said you had turned your back on us."

Rose stood up straight and sighed, "Yes, I guess to your mother's way of thinking, I did. But I wanted to make it right again. Forgiving me would be too easy, and perhaps you've noticed, your mother has never taken the easy road. Well, now maybe Sid will make things easier."

She led the way up the path, and Teddy followed, curious about the frank sadness in her grandmother's voice. "Yeah, but I don't think Sid makes much money," Teddy said, pursuing it.

They were now in the kitchen. Rose poured them each a cup of coffee and the conversation continued.

"So?"

"So, I think Mom needs more, you know, financial security. That'd give her an easier road, money would."

"She'll get security from me someday."

Ah, the words Teddy had longed to hear. Diplomatically, she replied, "Yeah, but she doesn't know that."

Rose smiled, some of her spark returning. "Now, there's a laugh. Nah Nah Stokes died a rich woman. Which means *I* will die a rich woman."

"I don't think Mom knows that. You never, I mean, I didn't think you and Mom . . ."

"Just say it, Teddy."

"Well, we were always so poor and everything."

Rose simply said, "Follow me."

She led Teddy into the library. She pulled a large hatbox down from a shelf and opened it. She handed Teddy one of ten batches of ribboned-up envelopes. Each one, addressed to her mother, had written across it, like the Christmas box upstairs, "Refused—Return to Sender."

"Open one," Rose commanded.

Teddy ran her finger under the envelope flap and pulled out a check for one hundred dollars, payable to Delores Ramsey.

"Here, how about one from thirty-eight?" Rose handed Teddy another, which she opened.

"All of them? A hundred bucks in each?"

"And each one returned unopened. So, if your mother has told you I never tried to help her out, well, now you know otherwise."

"Maybe she didn't know money was in these. . . ."

"She knew, Teddy."

"I guess that explains the Christmas box upstairs," Teddy said, letting it all sink in.

"I figured, if you found Nah Nah's ashes, you'd find those too."

"The dresses are too small," Teddy said, her eyes filling with tears.

"We'll exchange them," Rose replied, her own voice shaky but warm.

Teddy flipped through the envelopes and swiped away her tears. "I guess that means she chose her own rotten pride over us—over these." She rubbed her scarred hands.

Rose took those hands and held them in hers. "It took guts, not pride, to return all my peace offerings." She dropped Teddy's hands and went to the window to gaze out over the ocean.

"Mom wanted you, not the money?" Teddy asked carefully.

"If I hadn't stayed with that disgusting, dying old crone, my dear, sweet, departed mother, all her money would have gone to some bleeding-heart charity. Oh, something worthwhile, you may be sure. Like the Violet Society or, worse yet, some half-crazed political candidate. That's the kind of beast she was. Your great-grandmother was quite a piece of work. She kept me with her with that threat. She bought me."

Teddy held up a batch of envelopes and asked, "Well, isn't that what you were trying to do with Mom?"

"I don't think I'll ever get your mother to realize what I went through for that money. Nah Nah Stokes was a devil.

As mean and hard as they come. I remember, after the fire, when I told her I was going to Tacoma to be with my own daughter. . . . There she was, a tiny ball of steel in bed."

Teddy watched Rose as she seemed to be reliving that moment so long ago. " 'Don't leave me, Rosie. I'm dying. Don't let me die alone. Andrew and Francesca are dead. What can you do for Delores now?' Can you imagine a mother saying that? I told her I had to do something, anything, be there, hold her, help her, money, doctors, furniture, rebuild. . . .'"

Rose was again at the window, looking out. "My mother looked up at me and said, 'Rebuild? My dear, with what?' Oh, I knew what she was up to. Any chance I had of helping my daughter was through my own inheritance. I wouldn't have gotten a dime if I'd left my mother. You know what? I actually thought about putting a pillow over her face and killing her. I was this close." She held two fingers an inch apart. "But, well, I didn't. I stayed and waited. Your mother has hated me for it night and day ever since."

She walked over to the hatbox and touched the letters lovingly. "And the whole, god-awful irony is all in this hatbox . . . 'Refused—Return to Sender.' "

Rose pulled a hankie from her back pocket and blew her nose. "So you see, my dear, your mother could have walked in that door on the arm of Adolf Hitler and I wouldn't let it come between us. For ten years I've been trying to gain her forgiveness, and I'm sure not going to mess it up now."

"Mom's stubborn as a mule," Teddy said. "All you two do is fight."

"She sure holds one hell of a grudge, I'll give her that. Just when I think we're about to finally forgive and forget, we start bickering about something silly and before you know it—war."

"She's that way with everyone, Rose," Teddy said softly. "Hey, look, she took the C-note you had Howie slip her. And did you notice? She was wearing that good hose. It's a start."

Rose smiled at Teddy. "You know, if I have to buy every nod your mother ever gives me, I don't care. Every dime I spend on her, on you kids, cripes, even Sid now, buries Nah Nah Stokes a little bit deeper."

"Buries?"

"Oh, all right, scatters her ashes a little bit farther. That better?"

Teddy nodded and tried to find something else to joke about. But inside, she began to feel unsteady, uncomfortable. As though she had a restless itch somewhere inside her and she couldn't scratch it even if she could locate it. She needed to escape, before it was her turn to confess something. That was the way conversations like this went: I tell, then you tell. She had done such an expert job so far of diverting the pain, the plots, the ploys away from herself, and that was the way it had to stay.

No, all she had to do was think of a way to keep Howie together, keep her mother happy and distant, and of course, there was this little matter of arranging forgiveness for Rose that needed tending, not to mention constructing the Best Damn Dam of 1944.

She found a reason to leave the library, pried Howie out of the bathroom and went down to the stream.

Enough was enough.

TWENTY-THREE

Deep down inside, Teddy knew it was stupid to begin serious work on the dam, what with tides, winds, pillagers, squatters. August first was four days' worth of God-knows-what stream alteration away. But without the distraction of fishing, Howie needed something, anything, to do. It would be just like him, in his anger toward his mother, to waste away in the musty confines of the storm fort. Where was that girl he'd been hanging around with? What was her name? Amelia? Pearl? Brenda? Where was Amelia-Pearl-Brenda now that she was needed?

"All right. One more time, Teddy. Just because I'm a little bit fuzzy right now. You and Steve bet what?" Howie asked, splashing cool water from the stream on his ashen face.

"I bet I could build a better dam than him by August first." She handed Howie a shovel and added, "So start digging."

"You mean he builds one dam and you build another? What? That's stupid."

"No, no, you imbecile. He's going to build from that side

166

and me from this side. Whichever side holds back the most water for the longest wins."

"You're the imbecile, Teddy. Think about it. Whichever side is strongest will force water over the other side. It'll be over before it's a contest." Howie illustrated with his hands as though the dam were right there in front of them. "It's a stupid bet, Teddy."

"No, it's not. I'm building this half and Steve's building—"

"Here, snipe, snipe, snipe," Howie baited. "I keep telling you, Steve isn't going to waste his time building a dam. He's been pulling your leg all along."

"He tell you that?"

"Well"—Howie hesitated—"no, but Steve's too cool to play in the sand. This is kid's stuff."

Teddy didn't care. A bet was a bet. A dam was a dam. She picked up his shovel and shoved it into the sand just inches away from his bare feet.

"Dig!" she commanded.

He took the shovel and started to dig along the shore where Teddy had etched a foundation boundary with a stick. "All right, but just because there's nothing else to do. And something else, if any of the town kids come around, I'm throwing down my shovel. Besides, we'll probably all be back fishing tomorrow."

That reminded Teddy. "What sort of a family emergency?"

"Mom got married," Howie snapped. "Where've you been?"

"No, at Steve's."

"I don't know. Probably an aunt or uncle croaked. Maybe

167

the Japs hijacked their fishing boat. How the hell should I know?"

Teddy put down her shovel. "Harry! I'll bet Harry came walking down out of the hills!" Teddy looked toward the horizon, as though she could see Steve's adored Harry emerging from the jungles, rifle up, escorting hundreds of surrendered Japs.

"What the devil are you gibbering about? Harry who, Dini?" Howie laughed, for the first time that day, at his cleverness.

"Steve's brother. You mean you've been fishing with him all this time and he's never mentioned Harry to you?"

"Oh, *that* Harry. Sure, of course I know about Harry."

The brass bell clanged just then. "Ah nuts, just when I get started," Teddy griped.

"Does she have to clang that thing so loud?"

"Here, hide your shovel by these bushes. Come on. It's probably Mom on the phone telling us now she's pregnant." Teddy led the way up the path.

"Just since she's left? Can you tell that fast?" Howie asked, not warranting a reply.

It had been a phone call, only it wasn't from their mother. It was the local news-spreader, dutifully notifying all interested parties that Holiday Beach had lost another man to the war.

Rose thought the twins should know.

It was Harry Maloney.

The local kids gathered early on the beach that evening. The fire was up and snappy before the pink had faded into

168

the gray of the horizon. The guitars came out early, as though to avoid talk. Harry had not been a part of this crowd, but through Steve, they all knew him well. There had been something cohesive, something wildly optimistic in Steve's stories of Harry's war. Steve had convinced them all he'd come back—missing in action was sometimes just misplaced in action. According to the War Department and the local gossip that grew from the telegram, Harry had indeed been misplaced. Killed months ago, body mis-marked and mishandled, stored in San Francisco, until someone got around to matching toe tags to dog tags. And now, now they all knew their hero's hero, Harry Maloney, was coming back in storage. No more of Steve's marvelous stories of stunning survival, gorgeous native women and outsmarted Japs.

The mourning grew into the darkness as bottles were passed and toasts rendered. No, no one had seen Steve. No calls, no hot-rodding down Seaview, no pinball challenges. Teddy and Howie sat closer than they usually did during beach parties. But then again, this party was taking on all the characteristics of a wake.

"This is getting weird," Howie whispered to Teddy. "They all must have known the guy wasn't coming back alive."

"I'm game for leaving if you are," she whispered back.

Because it was early Saturday night, they walked to town, which seemed to be encased in a pall of its own. The fog bank had drifted ashore as though to veil the saddened eyes, keeping the local people safe, sheltered from the tourists.

The local theater was showing *Pinocchio,* and since it

was the height of the summer, Teddy thought it odd as she passed that the theater would be closed so early. Wasn't it only nine?

"Too bad. I could use a cartoon," Teddy said.

Howie tugged her sleeve and urged, "Come on. Maybe something's going on at the arcade."

But Teddy was busy looking inside the portal in the theater door, as though a darkened marquee and a big Closed sign in the ticket taker's window weren't enough.

"Somebody's in there," she said.

"Yeah, a puppet with a long nose. Come on, Teddy. Let's get something to eat."

But Teddy was knocking on the small window, trying to get the attention of the person inside. "Go ahead. I'm going to see if I can sit in on the ending. I love this movie."

"Suit yourself. But better be home by eleven-thirty or you know who'll come looking."

Howie left for safer ground. A few nickles into the nearest pinball machine and he'd practically be his old self again.

The theater manager finally tired of her tap-tapping on the window and opened the door.

"Closed," he said. But when the door opened, sound spilled out.

"Aw, come on. Can't I just catch the last? I'll pay full price."

The man looked out onto the street to make sure it was only one kid, and not a tourist mob, who wanted in, then opened the door wider for her to enter.

She offered him a quarter, which he refused.

170

"Keep it." He indicated the theater beyond and said, "Just sit in the back. Private party down front."

Teddy walked in, expecting rows full of rich little sticky-fingered, kid-tourists. She groped for a seat in the back row, took one and waited for her eyes to adjust to the darkness.

Then, as the light from the screen grew, she realized there was only one other person in the theater with her. He sat in the front row, looking up and laughing at the donkey-boys prancing on the screen above.

She slowly crept down, a few rows at a time, until she got a better look at the boy. A few steps closer and she knew it was him—Steve. How well she had come to know his laughter.

She looked down and saw empty beer bottles lined in a neat row on the floor in front of him. He laughed louder. She quietly slipped closer, knelt in the aisle behind him and wondered what in the name of God she was going to do next.

Finally, she laughed with him. He turned and saw her. Disney's wonderful magic light danced upon her face, and he didn't seem at all surprised to see her there.

She reached out and touched his shoulder and said, "Hey. Who's got the pain?"

TWENTY-FOUR

Steve's face smeared with a sloppy smile, half cartoon-crazed child, half drunk old man. "Hey, Teddy, who's got the pain? Here. This'll help." He handed her a warm beer, which she took, unsure why she shouldn't. "Want me to find you a seat?" He said, standing up and surveying the empty dark theater. "Oh, what luck. Here's a seat, right next to me."

He pulled her up and very formally assisted her to the seat next to him. He swept away spilled popcorn and peanut shells before she sat. He opened her beer for her, handed her the popcorn and looked back up at the screen.

As he put the bottle cap into his pocket, he said, "Save the Cap—Kill a Jap."

"Looks like you've killed a whole battalion," Teddy said, indicating the empties.

Steve grinned and asked, "How'd you find me?"

"I wasn't looking. Swear to God. I was just hoping to catch some of the movie."

"Well, you came to the right place. I plunked down a hundred bucks for this joint."

Teddy sipped her beer and watched the movie. As much as she adored *Pinocchio*, it wasn't going to make the situation any easier. What on earth was she doing here? Who was she to impose on Steve's agony? And Lord God, how was she going to get herself out gracefully?

"I . . . um . . . I heard about Harry. . . ."

"Did you hear he won't be coming back after all? My mistake." Steve didn't take his eyes off the screen as he talked.

"All the kids feel pretty awful."

"That beer cold enough for you? I got some cold ones up in the cooler."

"No, it's fine. I'm not much of a beer drinker anyway."

"I don't suppose you brought the flask?"

"Uh-uh . . ."

They watched more of the movie, and Teddy tried not to let her eyes wander to Steve's face. Finally, she spoke. "Guess what? My idiot mother went and got herself married." She tried to color her words to match Steve's agony, as though there could be any comparison.

"He a real jerk?" Steve asked, as though it was a stepfather prerequisite.

"I don't know. We just met him. Hell, Mom just met him. She probably doesn't even know if he's a jerk yet."

"Shsssss. Watch this part . . ."

They watched, laughed, passed the popcorn.

Teddy looked at the empty beer bottles stacked along the aisle and asked, "How long you been here?"

"This is the fourth run." Then he looked at her and cocked his head and added with a simpleton's grin, "I keep waiting for a different ending, but they keep running the same one."

"What do you mean? This has a great ending!"

"Too pat. I want 'em to use that cricket for whale bait." He looked at her seriously. "After all, I *am* a fisherman, you know."

They watched more of the film, and this time Teddy allowed it to pull her into the screen. Steve downed his beer, reached for another one and, still not taking his eyes off the screen, whispered, "I knew all along he wasn't coming back. I just said all those stories because, you know, the kids get some kind of a thrill thinking Harry's a hero or something."

Teddy felt a chill pass through her. This wasn't going to be easy. Steve talked weird when he was drunk and drunk he was. But rather than waiting for her reply, he popped up and ran up the aisle, calling back down, "I gotta take a leak. Need anything? Jujubes? Peanuts?"

"All set," she called back, feeling a little awkward talking above a whisper in a movie theater.

"Tell the puppet not to do anything till I get back!"

When he returned, it was with two more icy quarts of beer.

"Does your family know where you are?" Teddy asked.

"I'm a big boy. They know I'm around."

"Shouldn't a family be together at a time like this?" she dared to ask, the memory of Rose's hatbox filled with uncashed checks foremost on her mind.

"We'll be together Monday. That's when Harry's coming

174

. . . I mean, Harry's . . . body, is coming . . ." He started matter-of-factly, then each word built on the previous as he spoke until, by the time he said "body," his voice was low and heavy. He swallowed hard, stared at the screen and flexed his jaw. "They're letting Don, he's the one with Halsey, escort him . . . so, it'll almost be a . . . you know, a reunion. It'll be great to see Don. Bet he's got lots of stories. Mom's probably cooking already." Not once did he take his eyes off the screen, and as he talked, he seemed to react mechanically to the faraway fantasy unfolding in animation.

The movie came to an end, and no sooner had the credits begun to run when Steve stood up and hollered, *"One . . . more . . . time!"* Mr. Olsen appeared at the entrance and called down, "That's it, son. Let's pack it in."

Steve stood in the aisle, and as Mr. Olsen approached him, he swayed in the uneven darkness.

"I've already broken several laws tonight, Steve," he said kindly. He put his hand on Steve's shoulder and looked down to Teddy as he said, "Suppose you could get him home all right?"

"Aw, come on, Mr. Olsen. Just once more? Please? Tell you what, you set it up, and we'll clean up and put Pinocchio to bed when we're done."

"Now, Steve . . . ," Mr. Olsen said.

"Make a deal, just the first part, just the song, just the song. Then we'll go."

Mr. Olsen looked at Steve, then down at Teddy.

"Aw, come on," Steve persuaded, "let the bug sing."

"All right," Mr. Olsen said. "But just the first reel, you understand? You'll go home after that?"

"Right after the song," Steve promised.

"You'll clean all that up?"

"Sure . . ."

Teddy noticed Steve was swaying even more. How was she going to get him home?

Mr. Olsen left, and Steve stumbled back into his seat. He gave Teddy a cocky look and said, "See? I told you I own this town."

The movie began again, and Steve was held in its rapture like a little boy seeing the story unfold for the very first time. When Jiminy sat on the windowsill and stared out into the starry night, Steve leaned forward and craned his head up. Teddy watched him as he mouthed the words, occasionally slipping into a slight whisper, as the song evolved: "When you wish upon a star . . . makes no difference . . . dreams . . . come . . . true. . . ."

The last note echoed sweetly in the empty theater and was more beautiful to Teddy than ever before. Steve turned to Teddy, and the tears streaming down his face reflected the silvery screenlight.

Mr. Olsen stopped the projector, and the animation slowed until the creatures became silent still life, then vanished when the projector light went off.

"I never told him about Bluebird . . . ," was all Steve whispered as the darkness enveloped them.

Although Steve lived north of town, he pulled her along toward the south.

"Come on, Steve. Wrong way. You're going home," Teddy said, almost supporting Steve's bulky frame as he wobbled down the walk.

"No, come on. Let's hit the beach. The party must be getting a glow on by now."

"Naw, I don't think so, Steve. It's later than you think. Come on. I promised Olsen I'd get you home safe."

"Want me to drive?"

"No, I want you to walk and give me some warning if you're going to puke, okay?"

"I'm not going to puke, and I'm not going home. They'll all just be sitting around crying." He broke away from her grasp and started walking down the narrow, sandy passageway between two buildings toward the beach. Teddy pursued him.

But Steve pulled up short and faced Teddy when she reached for his arm. "Who the hell are you, anyway?" he shouted. "You come down here and think you own me!"

Nobody, drunk, sober or in mourning, talked to Teddy that way. She spit right back, "Look, jerk, the last person on earth I want to own is you! I know you're upset about Harry, but you're not the—"

"Wait a minute, I know the rest. . . . I'm not the first to have a brother get shot to bits and I won't be the last, right? God, you're *so* original! Oh, but I forgot . . . aren't you the one who fried her old man and baby sister? That's right, I'd forgotten! Great! So you *do* know how I feel!"

He was screaming at her in the passageway, his words reverberating back and forth, back and forth. Her face split with horror at his accusations, but, this time, her own words of defense failed.

"Then how come I don't feel any goddamn better!" he demanded, screaming even louder, without mercy. He shook her violently.

177

Teddy was choking with anger, terror. She was momentarily paralyzed; then she broke away from his grasp and ran for the beach.

"Teddy, wait!" he called out, running after her. She was cresting the first dune. "Teddy! Don't! You're the only one who knows how I feel!" It wasn't his words so much as the desperate pitch at which he shouted them. She stopped and allowed him to catch up to her.

They grasped each other and fell to the sand, holding one another tight, crying, "I'm sorry, I'm sorry, I'm sorry. . . ."

TWENTY-FIVE

Steve passed out and Teddy wouldn't leave him. Although they weren't far from town and adults and help, she opted to stay with him, keep him warm. She knew it was getting close to curfew, but with his head warm and heavy and trusting on her lap, she didn't seem to care.

He finally stirred, just as she was beginning to lose feeling in her legs. "Cold . . . ," he muttered.

"Come on, Steve. It's late. I got to go."

He opened his eyes, looked up at Teddy and whispered, "I'm sorry . . . what I said."

"Well, don't be."

"I promised Howie I'd keep my mouth shut. I'm sorry."

"Does the whole damn town know?"

"No, just me. He only told me 'cause I pushed him into it. Honest. I wanted to know how your hands got like that."

"Well, the next time you feel like pushing Howie, push him overboard, why don't you? He can barely swim, you know."

There. That helped a little . . . one betrayal for another.

But her dry comment was, apparently, a reminder to Steve, for he said, "Good brothers don't come easy. . . ."

"Go home, Steve," Teddy whispered down to him.

He sat up. "What time is it?"

"After midnight. I'm skeeee-roooood, you know."

Steve smiled wickedly, gripped his shirt collar and chastely said, "You didn't take advantage of me while I was out, did you?"

"No, but I thought about rolling you for quarters." She stood up and offered him her hand, which he took, and she pulled him to his feet. He wrapped his arms around her neck and held her tight. They rocked a little, and he whispered, "God, I'm glad you're here. Come on. I'll walk you home and stand fire."

"No. Rose'll understand. You get home. Don't leave your mom alone anymore."

She wanted it that way, walking back alone, on the beach, studying her own anger. How could he, Howard the Coward, tell Steve, tell anyone, about their hideous past? So much for promises, so much for Honors Bright. As mad as she'd ever been at him, this was the topper.

By the time she walked up the kitchen steps, she could feel her blood boiling. Howie needed a lesson—one he wouldn't forget for the rest of his life. If she was ever again going to trust him, it would now have to be a trust borne of fear.

"You know what time it is?" Rose asked, robed, coffee and cigarette in hand, at the kitchen door.

Teddy looked at her and said bluntly, "I was with Steve

180

Maloney. He got drunk, and I wanted to make sure he got home okay. I'm sorry. All right?"

Teddy's face must have matched her voice, for all Rose replied was, "Are you all right, Teddy? What is it?"

"Howard up?" Teddy asked back.

"Why? What's wrong?" She followed Teddy into the dining room and the living room beyond. There stood Howie, in his flannel robe, a cup of cocoa in his hands.

"So where were you?" he asked imperiously. "It's after one, you know." He sipped some cocoa, and as he did, Teddy walked up to him and with all her might slugged him in the stomach. He sprayed the room with cocoa as he doubled over, unable to talk.

"That's for every goddam Honor Bright you ever broke and don't you ever forget it!" she growled as she walked away.

Rose was too shocked to say anything.

"Night, Rose," Teddy said as she passed into the dining room.

JE125—Steve's brother, Harry the Hero, died. My brother, on the other hand, Howard the Coward, didn't die. Instead, he told. He told Steve about the fire. It's a good thing I didn't have a gun or that slug in his stomach would have been lead instead of my fist. Oh, I know Howie. He'll get to thinking about it and come crawling up, beg my forgiveness. He always does and I always do. I hate him!

The body, Harry's, not Howard's, arrives home on Monday. Mom and whatshisname will be back then too. Whoopee. Good day to work on the dam. I'll tell you this, from now on, Howie's on his own with that Sid.

She'd barely tucked the journal safely away when there came a knock on her attic door.

She walked to the door, unlocked it and said, "What kept you?"

Howie stepped in, rubbing his stomach.

"You really hurt me, you know."

"Just say it and get out."

"Say what?"

"What you came up here to say."

"I didn't come to say anything."

"Then get out."

She tried to shove him out the door, but he shoved back. "Quit it! I came to ask you how Steve's doing."

She held the door wider for him and said, "How would you be?"

"Drunk."

"Well, so's he. Now get out, Howie."

But he walked in farther and sat on a trunk. "You and me've had a rotten weekend, huh, Teddy?"

Here it comes, she thought—*The Big I'm Sorry.*

"Do you mind? I'm really tired, and I want to get an early start on the dam tomorrow." She wasn't going to let it be easy.

"I want to help with the dam, you know. I just don't know how much good I'll be with this knot in my gut. You really hit hard, Teddy."

"So see a doctor."

"You'll notice I didn't hit you back or yell or anything," he tried.

"That's because you knew I'd kill you!"

Howie simply stood up, looked directly at his sister and

182

said, "I would have deserved it. You could have kicked me to kingdom come and I wouldn't have done anything. I told. Look, Steve and me were drunk. You know how it is. I didn't even think he'd remember. I'd forgotten until to-night."

By now his words were slow and whispering. He walked to the door and added, "I guess it's just about the worst thing I've ever done."

She tried to let him get all the way out the door and have only her silent, cold stare to think about that night, but something inside her wouldn't keep quiet and before she knew it, she said, "It's not the worst thing you've ever done. But it's right up there."

He left to contemplate the fiery sting in his gut, and Teddy locked the door behind him. No, it wasn't the worst thing he'd ever done. The worst thing he'd ever done was play with matches under a Christmas tree in 1934.

TWENTY-SIX

By Monday, midmorning, Teddy's side of the stream had been seriously altered by the work she had done. Working all day Sunday, easy weather, easy tides, no interruptions, she had dug, hauled and placed a sturdy foundation. The stream, only partly dammed, simply took its course elsewhere, slightly north. She dared any tide, during any storm, to alter her engineering.

Under the circumstances, she doubted Steve would take his dam seriously . . . the death, the family, the funeral. But a bet was a bet, and besides, nothing in the rules said they had to stick to the deadline. She could be flexible. In a few days, Steve would need the mindless distraction of building a dam. So far, the distraction was working for her.

Howie had humbly hung around until she pressed him into service—not so much to bring him back into the family fold, but to cash in on his muscle. He hauled, dug, dumped . . . all without questioning her authority. She rudely took advantage of him, ordered him around—"Not here, there!" "Go for food!" "Do that over, it's not right!" But he was so eager to attain grace that she soon tired of it, and by noon, she managed to speak almost civilly to him.

She took his cola from his hand, sipped it long, then, looking at the half dam, said, "Dam good, if I say so myself."

"Look how much more the stream has gone that way," he said, pointing across the water. "You know Steve isn't gonna build his half, Teddy," he added cautiously. "Not now."

She looked him in the eye and replied coolly, "You think that kind of talk ever won a war?"

"This isn't a war, Teddy, it's a dam, for crying out loud."

Then they heard it, the downshift, the discordant diesel honk. The twins turned, and there was the truck, empty now of hay, turning left and approaching the bridge over the half-dammed stream.

Nowhere to run, nowhere to hide. Dee Dee was back, full-throttle, waving daintily out the window with Sid at her side and Perkie on her lap.

Teddy and Howie looked at each other, twin sighs, twin disappointment, twin disgust. Howie started trudging up the path and mumbled, "I mean it, Teddy. I'm not going back home. I don't care what Mom says."

"Then why are you going up to the house?"

"Because Mom's here," he answered stoically, as though Teddy were deaf and blind.

"She only left two days ago. It's not like she's been gone a year. Stay down here working on the dam. You go running up there the minute she arrives, she'll think she's got you again. Look, I know how to ignore Mom. Stay here and I'll go get us something to eat. Act cool."

"Tell her either I stay or—"

"Look, one step at a time. We can't all fit into that truck anyway. We gotta first talk her into letting us stay down for August. Then we'll start thinking about the rest of the year."

She spoke so assuredly, so logically, she was left with no alternative than to trust herself.

The honeymoon apparently over, Sid this time let Dee Dee climb down out of the truck by herself while he pulled out two small suitcases. Dee Dee looked like a calendar girl, yellow sundress, matching straw hat, sunglasses, standing on the running board, waving through the opened door at Teddy.

There she is, Teddy thought, *Miss Diesel of 1944.*

"Yoooohooooo, Theadorrrrra!" she called, as though Teddy hadn't noticed, heard, smelled their arrival.

Starting on her day of diplomacy, Teddy gave her mother a cool kiss, wondering what kind of cheap perfume she had gotten herself into.

"Here, Theadora. Poor Perkie has to gogetum. Would you?" Dee Dee handed her the leash and gave Rose the same chilly kiss Teddy had given her.

Sid paused on the walk and smiled down at Teddy. "Where's your brother?" he asked, looking around.

"Down on the beach."

"I got a ball and a coupla mitts in the truck. Thought we'd play us some catch."

"Sure," Teddy replied absently, trying to maneuver Perkie toward the ivy. "Howie's got a good arm."

Sid held back and said, "I got three mitts. Maybe, if your mom don't mind, maybe you'd join us."

"Yeah. Maybe. Come on, Jerkie," she said, pulling the dog along toward the road.

"Sii-id," Dee Dee called out from somewhere above. "I need my little blue suitcase."

Teddy brought Perkie into the kitchen, unhooked the leash and started to make sandwiches for herself and Howie. She heard the unmistakable clomp of her mother's high heels coming toward her and hoped she was alone.

Dee Dee walked to the fridge, pulled out a quart of beer, opened it and tossed the bottle cap into the garbage.

Teddy quickly retrieved it and said, disapproving, "Mom, 'Save a Cap, Kill a Jap.'"

"I hate that expression! You shouldn't say it."

"Everyone says it, Mom. It's patriotic," Teddy answered, placing the cap on the counter.

Dee Dee picked it up and looked at it in the palm of her perfectly white hand. "Gee, I hate to think of this as killing some Japanese mother's son," she said wistfully.

Teddy took it from her, plopped it into the scrap box under the sink and, thinking her mother's words quite profound for her, replied, "Don't worry about it. The war'll be over by the time this tin makes it overseas."

Dee Dee poured a glass of beer and offered Teddy a toast, saying, "Here's hoping you're right." She leaned against the kitchen counter and lit a cigarette. "So, how have you and Howie been?"

The smoke wafted gracefully and mixed with the sunshine streaming in.

187

"Since Saturday? Fine." Teddy knew by the curious absence of Rose and Sid, even Perkie for crying out loud, that Dee Dee had arranged this little time with her daughter.

"So, you like Sid, huh?"

Teddy simply replied, "He's all right, I guess. I don't know him."

"I do," Dee Dee replied, with the dreaminess of a sixteen-year-old prom queen. "He's swell, he really is."

Teddy looked at her mother's expression, paused for a moment, then said, "I hope you two will be very happy together," word for word like so much movie dialogue.

"Do you, Theadora? Do you really?"

There was something girlishly hopeful in her voice that made Teddy smile at her mom. Was that all it took? After all the years of haranguing, crying, bribing, lying . . . was that all it took? A simple, halfhearted wish for happiness? "Yeah," she replied, "I really do."

"Then you're happy for me?" Dee Dee asked, approaching. Teddy faced her fully, recognizing an impending mother-daughter moment when it came stalking. "Sure. Just so long as he doesn't, you know, try to change things."

Dee Dee stopped. "Like what?"

"Well, like Howie."

"How do you mean?" A long drag on her cigarette.

"Mom, Howie's been the man of the family for ten years. Ever stop to think he might be feeling a little, you know . . ."—she searched for a word her mother would understand—"upstaged?"

Dee Dee's face wrinkled as the thought passed through. "Oh. Gee. I never thought about that."

"Just tell Sid not to act too big around Howie, you know

188

what I mean? Maybe he can just settle in a little at a time." She took two apples from the cooler and placed them in the canvas lunch sack.

"Something else, Mom," Teddy continued, feeling very much in control of the moment. "I really think you and Sid need the rest of the summer to yourselves. Back home in Tacoma."

"Gee, that's funny, 'cause me and Sid were talking and Sid thinks, I mean, we think, well, if you kids really *do* want to stay here for the summer, then . . ."

"Then you'd just as soon be rid of us?" Teddy finished for her with a smile of budding victory.

But the look on her mother's face surprised her. "Oh no, not at all! Theadora, how could you think that? Is that what Rose said?"

"No, but, well . . . you *are* newlyweds."

"But that's not the reason at all. Sid said he understood how you kids might feel. You know, about him. Maybe you'd accept him easier if we let you stay here like Howie wants. Aw, gee, Theadora, I'll be so lonely without Howie and you with us, it's just . . ."

At least she'd accomplished her first objective—saving the summer for Howie—with little bloodshed. And, as it turned out, their mother had Sid to blame now if, for some reason, things didn't work out.

Teddy took a couple of colas from the fridge and added them to her lunch.

"Look, Mom," she said, heading for the door. "Can you do something for me? Let me handle Howie. Stay clear of him."

"But I'm his mother," Dee Dee said, almost helplessly,

almost as though she had to hear herself say it. "I don't want to lose Howie on account of Sid."

"You and Sid go home. Have some fun, huh? Come back down late August and we'll see." Teddy opened the screen door.

Sid walked in, and Dee Dee lit up in his presence. He kissed her and asked, "Can I steal a beer?"

Teddy said, "We're on the beach, Mom." And she carefully let the screen swing closed.

She paused on the last step long enough to overhear Sid.

"You know, Deed, Teddy's gonna be a real looker someday. Pretty as her mom."

Teddy didn't stick around for Dee Dee's reply.

TWENTY-SEVEN

Curious, but it appeared as though Norman Rockwell had set up his easel that afternoon . . . lopsided in the sand perhaps, but the scene was almost a cover for the *Saturday Evening Post*. Sunny beach, glittering ocean, kites, picnic, three generations. But it was only a pose, for none of them had much to say to the others.

Rose had laid blankets down, and Dee Dee had prepared a lunch of baloney sandwiches. Sid stuck several quarts of beer and a bottle of wine into the stream to chill and held true to his threat to bring down a ball and three mitts.

Dee Dee was stunning, teasing the sun in her green sunsuit, hat, sunglasses. She sat midblanket under the protection of a beach umbrella. Rose lay in the sun, full exposure, shorts and halter top. Sid had shed his workshirt and, in his sleeveless undershirt, with his muscled arms, looked considerably younger. Teddy laughed at his uneven tan— left arm nearly black up to his bicep; right arm as white as Dee Dee's dimpled knees.

Teddy and Howie kept their distance, kept working on

the dam. Howie stared at his mother and Sid, then asked, "You tell Mom I'm staying down here?"

"No, actually, she told me."

"Huh?"

"I mean, everyone thinks it's a good idea. Look, I took care of it," Teddy answered flatly, not about to disclose her talk with their mother.

"You mean she wants to get rid of us?" Howie asked.

"Look, it's what we wanted, remember? Who cares about the rest? So shut up and dig."

"Hey, Howie!" Sid called out from across the stream and down the beach. "How about some catch?" He held up the mitts as he called.

Teddy and Howie looked at each other, then back down at Sid.

"Go on," Teddy said. "Show him what you got."

"You come too."

"Sure. Why not?" They put down their shovels, tossed their gloves into the sand and waded the stream toward the adults. Sid tossed Howie a mitt. Teddy sat next to Rose and watched.

Sid threw the ball and *thaup!* Howie caught it with a surprised look as his mitt closed in on the baseball. He threw back at Sid, hard and direct and *thaup!*

A few more times back and forth. Each throw a little harder than the last.

"Now Sid, not so hard," Dee Dee cautioned.

"It's okay, Mom," Howie said, almost under his breath and sizing Sid up as a pitcher assesses the next batter.

Thaup! Thaup! Thaup! Thaup! Wonderful sounds . . .

sounds of strength and perfect follow-through, sounds of leather on leather, sounds of fathers and sons.

Each toss came harder, each catch louder. Teddy noticed the extra mitt on the blanket, and she rose to take it. But Rose held her back and said, "Not just yet, hon."

She sat back down and held the mitt, watching the baseball fly between them as though she sat center court in a tennis match.

Finally, Sid lost the ball . . . it tipped his glove, zinged upward and rolled toward the ocean. Howie looked at Teddy, and she gave him a silent thumbs-up. When Sid returned with the ball, Teddy had donned her mitt, and they formed a triangle. She knew they were, both Howie and Sid, catering to her, as the unwritten rules took over. She knew she threw like a boy, cripes, better than most, but she knew they were tossing her condescending, girl throws. Her anger grew with each easy catch, making her return the ball even harder.

Dee Dee signaled an end to the threesome by calling out, "Oh, Sii-id? Could you rub some sun lotion on my back?"

Sid kept the ball and walked back toward Dee Dee, followed by Teddy and Howie. They tossed their mitts on the blanket, having not said one word to each other the entire match.

"Come on, Teddy, let's get back to work," Howie said.

"Say, just what're you kids building up there? A bridge?" Sid asked, wiping sweat off his forehead and rubbing his shoulder.

"Just a dam," Teddy answered.

"Come on," Howie said, walking back across the stream.

"A damn what?" Sid asked, looking down at Dee Dee for an appropriate response to his pun.

"Sii-id," Dee Dee admonished sweetly, holding up the bottle of sun lotion.

But Howie had pulled Teddy away. Sid watched the kids go back to work on the dam. He followed, as Teddy had somehow figured he would. At least he was trying, she'd give him that.

He stood looking at the dam. "Which one of you two is the engineer?"

"Neither," Teddy answered. "We're just building."

"Where's the other half?"

"That's somebody else's problem." Teddy looked at Sid and realized the explanation might be too intricate for him. Sid looked toward the east and the hills that held the boiling clouds at bay.

"That stream ever swell?" he asked.

"Tides hardly ever come up this high this time of year," she explained knowingly.

"What about from that direction?" Sid asked, indicating the hills.

Teddy looked up, then back at Sid. "Huh?"

"What happens to the stream when the hills get a downpour? Doesn't the stream swell?"

"So what if it does?"

"You better plan a floodgate, 'cause if that stream fattens up some, you got overflow."

Howie, apparently tiring of the kibitzing, sliced his shovel into the streambed and said, "We know what we're doing."

But Teddy asked, "Floodgate?"

"Sure, over here, say." Sid walked a little upstream. "Water's got to have a release. Someplace to run off in case of that stream swelling. Sooner or later, you gotta think about a floodgate." He took a deep breath and added, "Smells like rain."

Teddy watched him as he spoke, trying to form an opinion. Then she said, "We're only messing around. I doubt that half'll ever get built, anyway. I don't think we need a floodgate."

Sid smiled and said, "You're the boss. But a dam without floodgates . . . don't think it's ever been done. . . ."

Howie stared coldly at him and said, "Hey, butt out, okay?"

"Only a suggestion, son." Sid caught his error and corrected himself: "Howie."

"What's a truck driver know about building dams?" Howie demanded.

Sid smiled a little and lit a cigarette as he replied, "You'd be surprised."

He walked away to help Dee Dee and Rose, who were packing it in for the day.

"What a creep," Howie grumbled, returning to work.

But Teddy was watching the clouds build in the east. "Yeah, but I think he might have a point. I never thought about a floodgate."

TWENTY-EIGHT

Rose had planned a weenie roast in the outside brick barbecue, even though the wind was picking up and the air had a smell of impending rain in it. Teddy kept her distance from the family, as did Howie. Even Perkie found a place to sit and watch. Sid had found the record collection, and he busied himself providing music to inspire the gathering: "Pistol Packin' Mama," "Praise the Lord and Pass the Ammunition," "Thanks for the Memory" . . . great war tunes all.

Howie ate and promptly excused himself. With the storm approaching, the kids would be gathering at the storm fort. As distracting as that escape sounded, as much as Howie tried to talk her into it, Teddy opted to stay home. After all, Steve wouldn't be there and . . . well, Steve wouldn't be there.

Besides, storms were wonderful from the attic, she'd discovered. She could look from her window seat on the puffs of the treetops and feel quite superior. The rain on the roof would beat its *tom-tom-tom*, then roll down and spatter on the windows of those less fortunate below.

Cocoa, a few records of her own choosing for the old player she'd unearthed, some journal entries of amazing brilliance and early to bed.

She heard the faint ring of the phone. Once, twice, three times before it stopped. She waited for steps on the stairs. It could be Howie calling from town, perhaps intent on getting her to change her mind. No matter, she wasn't budging.

She let out a breath of exasperated anger as she heard the door open from below. The creak of someone heavy on the steps. *Oh no, not Sid.*

"Teddy?" he called while rapping on the door. "You wanna take a phone call?"

"Is it Howie?" she called back.

"Nope. Steve Somebody. Wants to know if you can come out and play."

Teddy had to see the expression on Sid's face. She opened the door, and Sid was grinning, ear-to-ear, up at her.

"Steve Maloney?" she asked.

"You wanna take it or should I tell him to—"

"No, I'll take it." Sid started down the steps, and Teddy followed.

"Rose says you fixed the attic up real good," Sid said, uncomfortable perhaps in the narrow, dark stairwell with Teddy. "Mind if I poke my head in and look around? I'm an attic man myself."

Teddy paused, shrugged, said, "Nah, go ahead," and continued down to talk to Steve.

Their conversation was concise: "It's me, Steve. Can you get out? Good. Meet me at the bridge. Just say I wanted to take a walk. Five minutes."

That was it. He hung up. She scrambled back up the attic steps and startled Sid as he was looking at the sunset pinks through the window.

"Nice view," he said. "That the widow's walk?" he asked, pointing to the hatch.

"Yeah, but I wouldn't go up there, if I were you . . . it's real rickety."

"Okay," he replied softly. "You gotta date? Gonna rain."

Teddy grabbed her slicker and baseball cap. *Date? Did he say date?* "Nah, just meeting a friend, going for a walk."

"Steve?"

"Yeah, Steve."

"Need a few bucks? Kids your age oughta be going to a movie or bowling or something. Walks are for old geezers like your mom and me." He plunged his hand into his back pocket and pulled out his wallet.

"No thanks, Sid. We're just going to walk." She pulled on her slicker.

"Steve the boy whose brother died?" Sid asked casually.

"Rose tell you?"

"Uh-huh."

"Yeah, that's the guy."

He started walking toward the stairs. "You tell him I'm real sorry, okay? Tell him, if he maybe wants to talk, tell him I got two brothers laying on the bottom of the Coral Sea."

This struck Teddy as strange. Sid must be forty, maybe forty-five. She'd come to think that only kids got killed in the war. She followed Sid to the door. He turned, and she was struck by the peace in his face, the calmness in his eyes. He smiled and added, "Well, tell him it gets better, okay?"

He handed her two dollars and said, "You kids have some fun on me, huh? You head on out the back door. I'll tell your mom you're going out for a while."

She took the two dollars, thanked him with a small smile and went out the back door.

Steve stood on the bridge, leaning into the railing, looking down at Teddy's half dam below. His old truck was ka-chugging, barely clinging to its idle, at the side of the road. Approaching from the beach, Teddy climbed the rocks and, with Steve's help, pulled herself up onto the bridge.

"How's it going?" she asked him.

But instead of answering, he pointed to her dam, glowing now with the early evening sun, and asked, "You do that?"

"Yeah. Why?"

"Not bad."

"You mean, not bad for a girl?"

He looked at her and swung his arm around her neck and said, "Just 'not bad.'" He started for his truck. When Teddy hesitated, he said, "Come on."

"Where to?"

"Where all things end."

"You drunk?"

"Just a little."

"I'm not getting in that crate with you drunk."

He opened the driver's-side door and swept a long bow. "Then, ma'm'selle, I'm afraid you'll have to drive."

She hesitated, then climbed into the truck cab. She watched him swagger in front of the truck and whispered to herself, "I don't think I like this. . . ."

Before climbing into the cab, Steve reached into the bed of the truck and pulled out a big box. He plopped it onto the seat next to Teddy, then climbed in after it.

"What's that?"

"Open it." His face was glowing gold.

She undid the flaps and out popped the grinning face of a weimaraner puppy. Steve lifted the pup out and accepted the licks of joy placed upon his face. "Teddy, meet Bluest Bird. Bluest Bird, shake hands with Teddy." And he offered Teddy a big, soft paw, elevated his voice an octave and said, "Hello Teddy, how're you?"

Now, this *is a dog*, thought Teddy. She took Bluest Bird and allowed her to lavish warm puppy kisses on her face.

"Where'd you get her?"

"Vernonia."

"Oh yeah, pick of the litter."

"Drove all night and all day. Cashed in the voucher. Bluest Bird. Get it? Bluebird . . . Blu*est* Bird?" Steve took the puppy back and placed her in the box, this time allowing her head to poke out joyfully. Steve stroked the puppy's head and added, "Damn, Harry would have taught her how to fetch by now." He grinned at Teddy, then said impatiently, "Well, come on, let's go."

"Where?"

"North."

"Where north?"

"Seaside."

"All the way up there? What for?"

Steve slouched down in the seat and replied, "Because that's where Harry is, stupid."

Teddy watched Steve's face carefully. Was he drunk or beginning to crack?

"Steve . . . ," she began softly.

"Just drive, will you? Look, I gotta talk to him, you know? I just . . . I just gotta talk to him. Besides," he added with a cocky twist of his head, "Bluest Bird's been nagging me all day to meet him. Drive on, Thea-door." Steve pointed north. She hesitated, and he said, "You *can* drive, can't you?"

"Of course I can drive. It's just . . ."

"Then drive."

"But Steve . . . ," Teddy began. His eyes told her it was useless to try to talk him out of it. She felt an agonizing knot pulling tighter in her stomach. Even the curious, happily panting puppy at her side couldn't ease her foreboding.

Steve leaned toward her, touched her arm and said, "Come with me, Teddy. Please."

She slipped the truck into gear and started north.

TWENTY-NINE

Beck's Funeral Home was a lovely old building, white with green trim. The chapel entrance was serenely lit with gentle blue neon, and even in the darkness the approaching clouds brought, it looked quite undeathlike.

Teddy had every intention of waiting in the truck. She turned to Steve and told him so.

"Well, we can't go in yet," he explained. "Gotta wait till Mr. Beck locks up."

"Huh? You're family, Steve. Just go on in."

"You think old man Beck will let her in?" he asked, pointing to Bluest Bird.

"So, then how're you going to get in?" Teddy, feeling the impending intrigue, whispered.

Rather than answer, he held up a small, thin device, half penknife, half screwdriver.

"You're going to pick the lock of a funeral home?" she gasped, sorry she'd left the safety of her attic. "Isn't that . . . sacrilegious or something?"

"Come on, Teddy. It's a funeral home, not a church, for

God's sake." He held the lockpick up and added, "This baby was Harry's. It's picked many a lock over the years. Mostly just our old man's liquor cabinet, but it'll get us in there. Better pull around over there. We'll wait Beck out."

Teddy eased the truck around the corner, passing the dimly lit marquee, which announced Harry's funeral, 10:00 A.M., the following morning. Two gold stars held his name:

Harry Albright Maloney

Steve stared at it as they passed.

The lights went out at nine sharp. A wind was picking up from the east. From their back-alley hiding spot, they saw Mr. Beck lock the chapel door and walk next door to his own home. They waited for him to turn out his porch light before venturing farther.

"Steve, I'm not so sure about this," Teddy whispered as Steve got out of the cab, hauling Bluest Bird with him.

He turned and said, "You know, I was reading this story in *Time* magazine about how sometimes they ship the wrong guys home."

"Steve . . ."

"Well, hell, Teddy, they already botched it up once. It might not even be Harry in there." His voice was a little louder, and Teddy looked around to make sure they weren't being overheard.

"What do you mean, he might not be in there? Hasn't your mother seen him, for God's sake?"

Steve shook his head slowly. "They . . . the war guys . . . recommended a closed casket." His whisper was barely audible. "So, maybe it's not even him. . . ."

203

"Wouldn't Beck know?"

"Beck didn't do him. It's one of the bonuses of war. They do up their own dead. It's the least they can do."

Teddy knew it was useless to try to dissuade him. They snuck around to the rear entrance. Teddy held the puppy while Steve picked the lock. It was amazing how easily the door slipped open.

They stepped into the morgue, where the preparations were done. The foreign, acrid odors that greeted them made Teddy hesitate, but Steve pressed on toward a dim light beyond. The chapel.

There, in state, was the casket . . . waiting. All was ready . . . the American flag was draped across it, and a thin sentinel of light from a small spotlight overhead was shining down on it. Flower baskets were placed all around, each with gold stars sticking out as proud announcements that this man had died in the service of his country. Programs were neatly stacked on a chair. On a tripod placed center stage was a picture of Harry—uniformed, smiling, young, confident—he had Steve's eyes, Steve's smile.

The puppy, as uncomfortable as Teddy, squirmed in her arms, but Teddy didn't say anything. She petted the dog nervously and held her close, sinking into a front-row chair.

Steve carefully approached the bier. He ran his fingers down the entire length of the casket. He turned to Teddy and whispered, a gleam of hope in his eye, "I think Harry was taller. . . ."

Teddy, unable to speak, silently begged him to stop.

He undraped the flag—one fold back, two folds back, three.

He slowly, almost ceremoniously, began to unlatch the brass fittings that sealed the coffin. Each snap seemed to echo in the chapel, and Teddy prayed Beck would hear, come running and stop Steve.

Cla-kick!

Oh Steve, don't! Teddy screamed inside, holding the puppy now to her face.

Cla-kick!

Steve looked back to Teddy. "I've got to tell him something . . . ," he whispered apologetically.

Tears were streaming down Teddy's face, and Bluest Bird licked them off as fast as they formed.

He lifted the hatch.

"Oh God . . ." came Steve's horrified whisper. "Harry . . ." Then, lovingly, down at the soldier's face, an anguished, "I'm sorry. . . ."

"Close it, Steve," Teddy found herself saying, wondering where the authority in her voice had come from. She set the puppy down, walked bravely to the casket and slowly pulled the coffin lid back down over Harry, never taking her eyes off Steve's face. He was frozen, too weak, too horrified to protest. His knees buckled, and he sank down on the step. He laid his head on his folded arms and cried.

"Come on, Steve," Teddy whispered gently. "Let's go home."

The pup began sniffing about the platform, walked toward a spray of flowers at the casket's feet and started attacking a large lily.

"I hope she doesn't have to gogetum," Teddy said half seriously, trying anything to pull Steve away.

"Has to what?"

"Take a pee."

There was something incongruously funny about a weimaraner pup, all legs and feet, a lily petal sticking out of its mouth, large innocent eyes blinking, looking around for a place to pee under a flag-draped casket.

Steve smiled down at the puppy, and Teddy hoped the worst was over. Then Steve rose and touched the casket, ran his fingers lovingly around it and spoke down to Harry: "Say, that's some pup, huh, Harry? She's yours, you know. I mean, she would have been yours." His voice started to crack. "I . . . never told you this, Harry, but . . . it was me killed Bluebird." He paused as though hearing Harry chew him out. "Well, you *know* it was an accident. I was steamed about something and backed out of the driveway too fast."

Bluest Bird stepped closer to Steve, and he picked the pup up and held her close, like a kid who holds a precious toy at show-and-tell. "But look, I got you one just like her."

Teddy had to get out, get fresh air. "Harry says he forgives you," she said softly, touching Steve's arm.

"He does?"

"Yeah, didn't you hear him? Come on, Steve. Harry says, 'Go home now.' He understands."

Steve's face was red and anguished, but his eyes cast her a glint of hope. "He does? You heard him say it?"

"Sure. Just now he's saying, 'Don't worry about it. Go home and kiss Mom good night for me. Bluebird and me wanna go huntin' now. . . .'"

Steve smeared the tears off his face, smiled and said, "Yeah, that sounds like Harry, all right."

"Come on, Steve. Let's go." She pulled his sleeve to usher him along.

He put his arms around her, held both her and the pup, then walked them back out, through the morgue and into the storm-brewing night.

They returned, all the way from Seaside to Holiday Beach, in silence. Steve just stared out the window. Teddy kept her eyes on the road ahead. It had begun to rain, and the wipers only occasionally thunked back and forth, making the going slow and annoying.

Teddy drove to Steve's house and pulled the hand brake up tight and secure on the slanted driveway.

Steve ruffled the pup's ears and said, "Thanks, Teddy. For coming, I mean."

"Why don't you come by tomorrow and pick up your truck? I'll bet my mom's husband—I'll bet Sid—can fix those wipers for you."

"Yeah. A lot depends, on Mom and everything. You know how it is." He took her hand, which Teddy assumed he would shake. She was, after all, one helluva guy.

Instead, he put it to his cheek, then kissed it. Then he planted a huge kiss smack on the puppy's wet nose and said, "Be a good girl, Blue."

He opened the door but left the pup on the seat. "Hey, you forgot the dog," Teddy said.

Steve stuck his head inside, grinned broadly and said, "Oh, didn't I tell you? Harry thought you ought to keep her for him."

"Me? Why me?"

At this, Steve put his head back, allowing the rain to cleanse his face. To the heavens he called, "You hear that, Harry? She doesn't have a clue!" He shook his head in disbelief and said back to Teddy, "Just say, 'Thanks, Harry, I had a great time and I'll take good care of the dog.'"

She tried to get a better glimpse of his face in the dim light from the dash. Was Steve completely crazy now? Slowly she repeated, "Thanks, Harry, I had a great time and I'll take good care of the dog."

"Hey, and never let it be said ol' Steve Maloney don't show a girl a good time, eh?"

Teddy smiled back at him. "Wanna go knock over a few gravestones next week?" she answered.

He grinned, shook his head and replied, "Uh-uh—now *that* would be sacrilegious. Besides, I did that last week."

She knew he was going to be all right, from that moment on. He slammed the truck door and stood in the glow of the headlights while Teddy backed the truck around and drove toward home, Bluest Bird navigating from her lap.

THIRTY

It hadn't occurred to Teddy to wonder how she was going to persuade first Rose, then her mother, to keep the puppy. There was, after all, the little matter of a pouting Pekingese, who arrogantly flaunted a famous disgust for all other canines. But she was prepared to do anything, say anything, to keep this dog. It wasn't every girl who got a dog, pick of the litter, from the best breeder in Oregon, no less, and all on the say-so of a ghost.

She encouraged the pup to gogetum, then picked her up and entered the house via the kitchen. Only a light from the living room bled through as she tiptoed through the kitchen and dining room.

The cigarette smoke in the living room beyond lay low, like fog rising off a lake. It was her mother's voice that echoed first. "Well, to hell with that, Mother!"

Teddy turned and tried to escape back into the dining room. Too late. She'd been spotted. Perkie, up and alerted, barked obnoxiously at her and the curious cargo she was carrying. Perkie jumped up on Teddy's legs, running her perfect little catlike nails into Teddy's shins. It was nearly total reflex, but Teddy kicked the dog away as she struggled to hold on to Bluest Bird, who cried joyously at the sight of another dog.

Perkie yelped and came charging back for more.

"Mom! Get her!" Teddy yelled, defending herself.

"Perkie! Stop that!" Dee Dee called.

But it was Sid who walked over and picked the Pekingese up with a strong scoop. Perkie tried to bite him, and he simply held her out at arm's length. He handed the snapping menace to Dee Dee and said, "Here. Take this thing before I—"

"Sii-id," Dee Dee said, comforting her insulted dog.

"And who do we have here?" Sid asked, taking the puppy from Teddy. The puppy would much rather have played with the yapping little mop, but she found Sid's face a suitable distraction, and she licked it dutifully.

"Where'd you get her?" Sid asked.

"From a friend."

"Say, she's a beaut," he said.

Teddy knew she was about to win the dog war without ever even entering a puppy skirmish. It was almost too easy, but she asked anyway, "You hunt, Sid?"

"Bet someone spent a fortune for her," he said, setting her down and watching her plop herself into a sideways puppy sit. "Oh, she'll be a honey of a hunter."

"Theadora!" Dee Dee began, now struggling herself to contain Perkie. "That's okay, my liddle Perkie-Werkie. Mommy has you. Theadora, where on earth did you get that thing?"

210

"I said. From a friend. And I'm keeping her."

"Well, I rather think not, young lady. Since when do you go dragging home strays?"

"Mom," Teddy said forcefully, "I'm keeping this dog. It won't be any skin off your nose. I'll train her and pay for her food. Do you mind, Rose?"

But Bluest Bird had conquered Rose as well. Rose was petting the pup, now at her feet. "Oh, it's okay by me."

"Theadora, I said no," Dee Dee insisted. She handed Perkie to Sid and asked, "Would you, sweetie? I think all this excitement makes her have to gogetum."

"Again?"

"Please?"

Sid leashed the dog and obediently took her outside.

"What's gotten into you?" Dee Dee asked Teddy, a sharpness now in her voice. "You don't even like dogs."

"I like that one, and I'm keeping her."

"Oh come on, Dee Dee," Rose said, placing her hand on her daughter's shoulder. "What harm?"

"I'll tell you what harm. What about Perkie, *my* dog?" Dee Dee screeched. "That thing will grow to be huge and probably *kill* poor Perkie. Really, Theadora, dragging home strays."

"Well, Mom, you brought Sid home," Teddy said, confident, cool and cruel. She didn't know why she said it. She liked Sid. She really did. But, as always with her mom, the words were out before the thought had jelled.

Dee Dee's face reddened so brilliantly, so fast, Teddy wondered if she was maybe old enough to suffer a stroke. Then, oddly, her face softened, and she laughed lyrically. "Oh well, I guess that's true," she said.

Rose, caught as far off guard as Teddy, simply shrugged. It was as good an explanation as any.

Teddy, a field marshal who knew a victorious retreat when she saw one, scooped the puppy up and said, "I gotta get to bed, you guys. Don't worry, Rose. I'll set papers down for Bluest Bird."

"Who?" Rose and Dee Dee asked together, sounding, really, quite harmonious.

"You can call her Blue."

"Silly color for a dog," Dee Dee said, looking doubtfully at the puppy. "I'd call it Smokey."

"Blue," Teddy corrected.

It was no surprise to her that she couldn't sleep that night. She didn't open her journal, knowing that reliving the events of the evening would only haunt her until sunrise. She wanted to forget, for now at least, that it had happened, so that the memory of it could come alive another day . . . when maybe she could begin to understand. If it weren't for Bluest Bird at her side, she could nearly convince herself it hadn't even happened.

Blue settled down in her box next to Teddy until a door slammed below. Then her head cocked awake, and she alerted Teddy with a small what-was-that growl. Teddy looked at her clock: 11:30. Howie.

From then on, Blue kept her awake. Sniffing, snooping, clicking along the wood floors, whining for warmer sleeping arrangements. Teddy finally acquiesced and pulled the puppy into her couch-bed with her. But Blue was ready to play, not sleep.

The wind outside was beginning to howl, and the rain

pelted the roof, adding to their restlessness. The adults downstairs had apparently tabled all arguments, for the house seemed dark and settled and serene under her.

"I suppose you have to gogetum," she mumbled to the puppy.

The pup seemed to smile back.

"All right. Wait." Teddy put her slicker on over her flannels, pulled on a pair of knee-high boots and added her baseball cap. "But you better make it fast."

She carried the puppy downstairs and stood dutifully under the eaves as the puppy finally figured out what the midnight outing was for.

Once inside again, Teddy toweled the puppy off and wandered through the empty rooms, loving the feeling of having the house to herself. She paused in the living room, and her eyes came to rest on the piano. She sat and began to pick out melodies. It wasn't long before "Beyond the Blue Horizon" turned into *"Clair de lune"*—a natural progression from blue to green to *clair de lune*.

She played with the mute pedal to keep the music to herself. But it was no good, for her mother came creeping downstairs, resplendent in her flowing peignoir of white. Teddy knew she was there, somewhere behind her, listening. But she kept on until the last notes fell away and slipped gently into memory.

"You've been practicing," Dee Dee commented.

"Not much. Sorry if I woke you."

"Ah, I couldn't sleep anyway. Sid's snoring. Can't get used to it."

"Guess you'll have to."

"Guess so. Would you play that again?"

" 'Clair de lune'? You always came unglued when I used to play it."

"Well, you play it much better now, Theadora," Dee Dee stated, sitting down and allowing the puppy to sniff the delicate folds of her flowing gown.

Teddy started to play and dared to say, "Thought this reminded you too much of . . . well, the old days." Her mind flashed on Harry's flag-draped casket.

Dee Dee lit a cigarette and thought while she exhaled. "It does. But sometimes, everywhere you go . . ." She stopped.

"What?"

"Oh, you know. Who can ever get over such a thing?"

Does she know who she's talking to? Teddy silently asked the piano keys in front of her. Yet she thought of Steve's tears and pressed on. "Rose says a day at a time. Forgive. Forget. You know, the F-words." She stopped playing and looked directly at her mother, who was leaning back, staring at the ceiling.

"Oh, I forgave you years ago, Theadora," Dee Dee replied wearily, almost impatiently. "Keep playing."

Teddy didn't believe it for a moment—like someone who, over and over and over, tells you something so much its sincerity is lost in the repetition.

"What about Rose?"

"Oh, she's forgiven you, too. I'm sure, or else she wouldn't tell me such great things about you."

"I mean, you and Rose. Know what I think?" Teddy ventured cautiously.

She rose from the piano and looked down at her mother, who seemed more interested in squashing out her

214

cigarette than in what her daughter might possibly have to say.

"I think you're forgiving the wrong person, Mom. Why don't you let Rose know it's over?"

Dee Dee looked up at her daughter, and there was something comically lost in her expression . . . half here, half there, never totally in one place. Then she turned her gaze toward the puppy, and she said in a low voice, firmly, "I can never forgive her. She deserted us, you know. Some things can't be forgiven. Why, what has she told you?"

"That she loves you, that's all. She'd do anything to earn your forgiveness."

"You're just a child, what do you know about this? It's none of your business, anyway," Dee Dee said defensively, her usual parental tactic when the going got rough.

"I know a helluva lot more than you think, Mother."

"Watch your mouth, young lady!"

"I tell you what, Mom," Teddy said, "I'll forgive you if you'll forgive Rose. Deal?"

"Shut up, you're talking nonsense. *I'm* your mother. *I* don't need forgiving! No matter what *I've* ever done, it's been for *your* own good. Don't *you* tell *me* you'll forgive me! *I'm* your mother!"

She was pacing the room now as she spoke. Her gown flowed elegantly around her legs as she whirled around the room.

"Well, Mother," Teddy said bluntly, walking past her and picking up the puppy, who was chasing the tail end of Dee Dee's gown. "Here's a good-night thought for you"—Dee Dee stopped pacing and looked at her daughter—"I didn't start the goddam fire. Howie did."

215

For years she'd dreamt about throwing those words in her mother's face. Years of practiced, perfected dialogues, complete with tears, rage, followed by her mother's pleading, her anguished begging for forgiveness. Oh, it was all going to be very wonderful, the day Teddy told her mother that her own sweet, unscathed Howie was playing with matches that night. And that her hands, those scarred, sacrificed, perpetually gloved hands, had tried in vain to slap it out.

But somehow, that evening, Dee Dee in her gown of white and Teddy holding Bluest Bird, it hadn't turned out quite as she'd planned.

THIRTY-ONE

Dee Dee grabbed her daughter's arm as she passed, and whirled her around forcefully.

"What the hell did you say?" she demanded, her dimples now deep and determined.

"You heard me."

"I want you to say that again!"

"Howie started the fire!"

"I don't believe you!"

"I don't care if you believe me or not." Teddy's heart was pounding inside her. Was she saying this out of hate? Did she really hate her mother all these years? The tears in her eyes said no, not hate, not really.

"I'm sorry, Mom," she whispered, running her face down the pup's warm neck. "Don't you see? You're doing to me what Rose did to you."

"Rose abandoned us when we needed her most!" Dee Dee shot back.

"Just like you abandoned me after the fire, Mom," Teddy

217

replied, quite calmly. The words came easily, as though she had said them every day of her life.

"That's absurd! How dare you stand there and accuse me, your mother, of what? Lying? The truth hurts, Theadora! You know what happened! Just one day before the fire, Christmas Eve, remember? I spanked *you* for playing with matches!"

"It was Howie, Mom." She set Blue down and added through clenched teeth. "You caught *Howie* playing with matches!"

"You're confused, Theadora. I remember everything. The firemen, after the fire . . . they found matches . . . they asked about you children. I remember you playing with matches. I . . . remember? Someone was playing with matches."

"Not me. Howie!"

"Oh God, why does it matter who—"

"How could you hate me that much, Mother?"

"Oh no," Dee Dee cried, looking into Teddy's eyes with horror, "you're the most . . . precious thing in the world to me. . . ."

But Teddy wasn't hearing it. Her voice grew low and vile and threatening as she said, "And if you ever, *ever*, let on to Howie about this . . ."

"Howie?" Dee Dee asked helplessly.

Teddy seized her mother's wrist, not violently, but to make sure Dee Dee looked her in the eye. "Howie has no idea. And it's going to stay that way. I take the blame for Howie's sake. You ever tell Howie, I'm out of your life."

Dee Dee, shaking, slipped onto the sofa, ignoring the puppy rolling at her feet. "Howie doesn't know—"

"How could he? All our lives you've blamed me—"

"But I never . . . No, no, you're wrong. You were . . . I distinctly remember—"

Teddy cut her off. "Well, Mother, you remember it wrong." She held her mother's shocked and frightened gaze. Then she scooped the puppy up and brought it to her face, as though the wiggling creature could ease her heart as she asked, "Why me, Mom? Why'd you pick me?"

Dee Dee looked at her hands in her lap and answered almost in a whisper, "I was in shock. Such shock. It was after they'd taken you to the hospital. The firemen kept asking me what happened. Oh God, I had to choose one of you. I never meant to . . ."

"Why *me*, Mother?" She looked now into her mother's eyes.

Dee Dee didn't answer at first. It was as though the words wouldn't come, as though, after ten years, her lips weren't capable of forming the sounds. She swallowed, blinked out a rush of tears and finally said, "Because you were strongest. Oh God, because you were always so strong. From the very beginning, strongest. I didn't mean to blame you, Teddy. I just couldn't stand blaming myself."

Teddy looked into her mother's face. Had she ever called her Teddy before?

Dee Dee rose and approached her daughter and said, "After all, your father never smoked. Those were my matches. I'm sorry, Teddy, I'm sorry, I'm sorry . . . I'm sorry . . ."

Dee Dee reached out for Teddy and held her tight, puppy and all.

They cried and held each other until Bluest Bird, quite

219

obviously fed up with human emotions that night, yelped for freedom.

Teddy sat back, leaving the puppy in her mother's lap. No, it was nothing like Teddy had planned for all those years. It was better.

That night it was a warm hug good night, an embrace really—not just the cool kiss on cooler cheek. Teddy ascended, carrying the puppy, and entered her attic domain. There, on her sofa, Nah Nah's shoe box . . . open, empty. Inside a note:

Teddy—I heard you and your mother fighting. But I thought you should know, Nah Nah's on her way to Tahiti via the scenic route. I figured, if you could do it, so could I. No matter what, I love you.

Rose

JE126—Laid a few things to rest tonight. Promise more later.

Bluest Bird saw to it Teddy was awake and up by six the next morning. After a quick gogetem, Teddy scrambled back up the attic steps. She paused in front of her mirror and closely inspected her face. *Damn! Two pimples. Period must be coming.* She felt changed after last night. How come she didn't look changed? "What were you expecting, Dorothy Lamour?" she grunted at herself after extinguishing the pimples.

From there, she went up to the widow's walk to survey her beach, her stream, her dam, after the night's blustery weather. The fresh air engulfed her, and as always, she startled some seagulls off their perches.

220

Looking through the telescope down at her stream, she became worried as she saw how much larger, thicker, more swollen it was. Sid had called it, all right. But her side of the dam was doing a damn fine job of controlling its half of the stream.

"Rose says breakfast," Howie called up from the attic steps. He poked his head through the hatch to the widow's walk. He was greeted by Blue, always anxious to meet a new friend.

"Hey, where'd you get this?" he asked, enchanted by the pup.

"Long story," Teddy mumbled. "I'll tell you when you're older."

"Shut up."

He pulled himself onto the walk and sat, allowing the dog to jump for his nose. "You buy it?"

"Nope," Teddy said, still looking through the telescope.

"Who gave it to you?"

"It's a her, not an it."

"Okay, who gave *her* to you?"

"Harry did, not that it's any of your business."

"Who?"

"Did I say Harry? I meant Steve."

"Why'd he give *you* a dog?"

"His mom wouldn't let him keep her." It was so easy to lie to Howie.

"What about Mom?"

"She didn't want him to keep her, either."

"God, you're a jerk."

Teddy looked down at him and said, "Remember what happened last time you and me got into it up here?"

"Yeah, I pulled your fat ass back up here. *What* was I thinking?"

"Go suck an egg." She trained the telescope north toward a small puff of smoke coming from a sand-dune horizon.

"Make me," he replied, as the rules clearly stated he was required to say. "So, what went on here last night? I miss any good fights?"

Teddy smiled but kept gazing out at the horizon through the telescope. "Not much. Same ol' shit."

"Mom say any more about us staying down here to go to school?" he asked, rolling the puppy back and forth by massaging her plump, hairless tummy.

"I'm glad you're sitting down, 'cause I got news for you."

"What?"

"I think I like Sid."

"Benedict Arnold."

"You only don't like him because you think that's your job. I think he's all right. Think Mom drew a winner. I really do."

"Easy for you to say. Well, if he's so great, how come he's not in the service, huh, Teddy?"

Teddy casually replied, "Oh, I don't know . . . three years building roads and bridges from India to China, I'd say he's served his time—"

"The Burma Road? He tell you that?"

"No, Mom did."

"When?"

"Last night."

"Is that what all that racket was?"

Teddy didn't look at him but said, "Hope we didn't keep you awake."

"Nah, I threw my dirty clothes on the furnace grate so I didn't have to listen to you and Mom have it out. I heard it all a million times, anyway."

Teddy smiled into the telescope, then added, "Look, Howie, about Sid. All I'm saying is I'm going to give the guy a chance. I'm not going to run out and change my name to, what is it, Spirk, for crissakes." She turned the telescope and was now looking at Howie. "Jeez, you gotta lotta freckles."

From there, she turned the telescope back north to investigate the smoke puff, which was now blacker and seemed to be approaching them.

"Now what do you suppose that is?" she asked.

"What? Lemme see."

She allowed Howie a look. "I don't know," he said, "some kind of backhoe or tractor or something. Come on, Teddy. Rose is cooking pancakes." He released the telescope and started down the hatch steps.

"Howeeeee," Teddy said, watching the machinery approach up and over, down and through the sand dunes. "I'd swear that's"—she looked up, face blank, eyes surprised—"Steve."

"Huh? What about him?"

"Howie, what day is this?"

"A . . . Tuesday, why?"

"I mean the date."

"I don't know. Oh, August first. Why?"

Teddy didn't wait for an explanation. She grabbed Blue and her brother and said, "Something big's gonna happen!"

"What? What?" Howie called down after her. "She have to gogetum? What?"

THIRTY-TWO

Teddy had alerted the household, Perkie and all, to follow her. Coffee in hand, robes secured about them, the family followed . . . down the path, to the ridge, down onto the sand.

By the time they reached the stream, the sound of the chugging could be heard clearly, then more than clearly, then crashingly.

Steve, in the cab of an old, rusty bulldozer came chugging over the horizon, looking like a tanked-up Patton searching for one last desert rat to squash.

He stopped, idled his machine, got out and called out across the stream to Teddy. "What's the date?"

"August first!" both Teddy and Howie called back.

"That's what I thought!" He then forded the stream to its center, looked up at the half dam, licked a finger to test the breeze, sighted the center with his artist's thumb, then climbed back into the dozer.

Slowly, with great ceremony, almost as a salute to the spectators, the giant scoop, filled with large boulders, lowered. Smoke sput-sputted out of the exhaust as Steve bid the great old machine forward. He dumped the bulldozer's load into the stream. Then he backed up and pushed huge mounds of sand effortlessly into place.

Teddy and Howie's amazement had developed into a childlike enthusiasm for the instant dam. Their own hours of work, the blisters, the planning, the sunburn, the calluses, the aching muscles, were ancient, unimportant history now as Steve built his half of the dam before their very eyes.

Although the stream was nearly double today what it was yesterday, the deed was done in only a few moments.

Others, curious onlookers from the beach, had come up to see what was happening. Of all the adults, only Sid was grinning.

Finally, Steve shut the monster off and surveyed his handiwork. He walked to the stream, and Teddy walked along the top of her side of the dam to greet him in the middle.

He looked up at her, frowned dramatically and said, "I don't know . . ." He scratched his head. "Something's just—not right." He looked around, found a small rock and walked across his dam and placed the rock in the middle.

"There."

Already the backwater was rising closer, closer to the bridge.

"I guess you win, cheater," Teddy said, trying to be tough, yet unable to hold her grin.

"Not yet," he said, pointing to the bridge.

"That water's going to come over the bridge!" a concerned adult onlooker warned.

They watched as the water rose. Already Teddy could feel

parts of the dam erode away as the confused stream tried to break loose from its confines.

"Come on, come on, come on . . . ," Steve said, watching as the water inched higher.

By now, Howie and Sid had climbed the rocks toward the south side of the bridge to watch the water rise.

"Almost . . . almost . . . almost . . . ," Sid announced.

"You can do it . . . ," Teddy said, coaxing the water. After all, she should know. She and this stream had been quite intimate over the last several weeks. "You can do it."

The dam was beginning to crumble. Steve and Teddy nearly lost their balance as a large plank started to move, and they scrambled toward the shore.

"It's coming!" Howie hollered from the bridge. "It's gonna make it!"

"To hell with floodgates!" Sid cried, throwing his head back and laughing.

"Sii-id," Dee Dee called out, confused, from the path.

"Two more inches!" Sid called back, holding up two fingers.

"Go! Go! Go! . . . ," Steve chanted, soon joined by Rose, and finally Dee Dee. Perkie and Bluest Bird barked out their own encouragement.

"Yes!" someone, a stranger, called to the crowd.

"It's touching!" Howie screeched. "It's touching the bridge! She's gonna flood!"

Sid grabbed Howie away from their dangerous perch. The water foamed even higher to the bridge, to the curb, over the curb and deliciously over the road, only to cascade down the other side.

Teddy and Steve enveloped each other in jumping cheers. Then, with a decided *crack!,* the anchor plank gave way, snapping in half in the arms of the cascading waters. As though to say, "All right, you clowns, you've had your fun," the stream gushed over the dam, Steve and Teddy's dam, and with it carried the cords of stolen wood, the mountains of rocks, the hours of work. Back down to the ocean, where it all belonged.

Dee Dee and Rose watched as Teddy, Howie, Steve and even Sid whooped and hollered over the water's victory. Dee Dee said, "Look at that, will you, huh? My daughter—the Dam Queen."

Rose replied, her voice soft, her face full of admiration, "Yes, but isn't she something?"

Dee Dee looked at her mother, then back to Teddy. "Sure is."

Steve pulled Teddy away from the water's edge.

"Hear it?" he asked.

"What?"

"Harry's laughing his guts out."

Teddy looked toward the horizon and listened, then whispered, "Oh yeah."

"Hey, I gotta get that dozer back before ol' man Harding wakes up," Steve said.

"I'm building another dam tomorrow, you know," Teddy said, a challenging grin on her face.

"Any moron can build a dam. Changing the course of a stream—now *that* takes *real* talent."

Teddy glanced up at Sid, smiled back at Steve and said, "You're on."

She offered Steve her hand. As he'd done the night before, he kissed it gallantly.

Teddy slowly extracted her scarred, blushing hand.

"September first, shall we say?" Steve asked.

"Take as long as you need."

The moment was broken by her mother's anxious, high-pitched voice. "Yooooo-hooooo, Teddy . . ."

"That's my mom. I better go see what she wants, or she'll just stand there yoo-hooing all day."

"I'll call you after the funeral."

Teddy, wet, sandy, exuberant, waded across the stream to her mother and Rose as they watched the flotsam and jetsam of the summer cascade by.

"You spend the whole summer building that dam, only to let it all flood over," Dee Dee said, brushing sand from her daughter's face. "I don't get it."

Teddy and Rose looked at each other. They got it. It was as obvious as Dee Dee's freshly plucked eyebrows. They looked at Dee Dee and broke out laughing.

"And just what is so damn funny, huh?" Dee Dee asked, her hands instinctively going to adjust her hair under the pink scarf.

"You are, Mom," Teddy said, putting an arm around her shoulder.

Rose threw her arm around Teddy also, and the three stood, one moment in time, arm in arm in arm. With Teddy diplomatically, protectively in the middle, they watched as Steve got back into the hijacked dozer.

He stood up in the cab and saluted the family as the dozer chugged by. Teddy stepped forward and returned the salute, which left Rose and Dee Dee, quite accidentally, arm in arm. To Teddy's surprise, they stayed arm in arm as they turned and walked back toward the house.

"Well, I'll be damned," Teddy muttered as she watched them disappear up the path.

It wasn't peace in Europe. It wasn't peace in the Pacific. But it was a start.